NEAR OPEN WATER

ACKNOWLEDGEMENTS

These stories previously appeared, several in different form, in the following publications: "In the Atlantic Field" in *The Antigonish Review* and *Wasafiri*; "The Marches of Blue" titled "Under the Blue" in *Caribbean Beat* and *Journal of Caribbean Literatures*; "The Visitors" in *Mississippi Review* and an excerpt titled "The Vultures" in *The Trinidad Sunday Express Literary Section*; "In the Cage" in *Trinidad and Tobago Review* and *Short Story*; "A Landscape Far from Home" titled "The Nature of the Beast" in *Caribbean New Voices 1* and *Trinidad and Tobago Review*; "Caribbean Honeymoon" in *Tell Tales 4: The Global Village*; "Kanaima, Late Afternoon" in *Atlanta Review* and *Trinidad and Tobago Review;* "The Jaguar" in *Trinidad Noir*; "Night Rain" in *Atlanta Review*, *Trinidad and Tobago Review*, *Caribbean Review of Books* (website); "Fire in the City" in *Wasafiri*; "The White People Maid" in *Moving Worlds*. I'm grateful to the editors and staff of these publications for their assistance.

For their encouragement over the years, guidance, and insights on some of the stories in this book, and for helping to pluck time from the stars, my deepest thanks and appreciation to Anne Jardim, stellar composer of Boston red wine evenings; Pamela Gordon, Kevin Miller, Stratis Haviaras, Pam Painter, James Randall and DeWitt Henry of Emerson College; George Lamming, whose intellectual grace and generosity will always be remembered; Wayne Brown, whose love of islands, writing and literature was one of the best things to happen in Trinidad and Tobago; Lloyd Best, in whom the beauty of Western Civilization reigned triumphant; Jon Morley, for sound editorial advice; Rahul Mitra, for a wonderful and timely suggestion; Frederick Busch, for recognition that helped me cross oceans; Ken Ramchand, superlative reader, dear friend and Maker of Caribbean Light.

At the University of Houston: Lois Parkinson Zamora, whose words after reading an early version of this book I will never forget; Daniel Price, superb scholar, gentleman, and a funny man, too; Chitra Divakaruni, lady of light touches; Roxanna Robinson, lady of hearts; Adam Zagajewski, whose words after reading an early version of this book I will also never forget; James L. Kastely, Director of the University of Houston's Writing Program and one of the great humanities professors in our time.

Special thanks to Jackie Hinkson for the cover – his genius and generosity are much loved; to Victor Blackburn, for his photography; to Hannah Bannister for the detail; and to Douglas H. Chadwick for his article on jaguars, "Phantom of the Night."

And finally, my agent, Timothy Wager – gentleman, superfine critic and maestro of patience.

NEAR OPEN WATER

STORIES

KEITH JARDIM

PEEPAL TREE

First published in Great Britain in 2011
Peepal Tree Press Ltd
17 King's Avenue
Leeds LS6 1QS
England

ISBN13: 9781845231880

Supported by
**ARTS COUNCIL
ENGLAND**

In loving memory
of my father
Peter Jardim
26th May 1935, Guyana
7th February 1988, Trinidad
for his generosity
love of adventure
love of natural history
and for the democracy of his library

And for my mother, Corinne Jardim, nee Bettencourt,
with love and thanks, for her support

"You should have heard him say, 'My ivory.' Oh yes, I heard him. 'My Intended, my ivory, my station, my river, my –' everything belonged to him. It made me hold my breath in expectation of hearing the wilderness burst into a prodigious peal of laughter that would shake the fixed stars in their places. Everything belonged to him – but that was a trifle. The thing was to know what he belonged to, how many powers of darkness claimed him for their own."

– *Heart of Darkness*, Joseph Conrad

"'Do you know what you've done to me? It's not the girl, not the girl. But I loved this place and you have made it into a place I hate. I used to think that if everything else went out of my life I would still have this, and now you have spoilt it. It's just somewhere else where I have been unhappy, and all the other things are nothing to what has happened here. I hate it now like I hate you and before I die I will show you how much I hate you.'

Then to my astonishment she stopped crying and said, 'Is she so much prettier than I am? Don't you love me at all?'

'No, I do not,' I said (at the same time remembering Amelie saying, 'Do you like my hair? Isn't it prettier than hers?'). 'Not at this moment,' I said.

She laughed at that. A crazy laugh."

– *Wide Sargasso Sea*, Jean Rhys

CONTENTS

IN THE ATLANTIC FIELD

The boy, whose mother is driving, is nine years old. He looks at strewn rocks on the beaches below, afternoon sheen on watery sand, and the sky, a blue almost uncanny in its purity. Cool wind lashes the car.

Earlier, they had passed a village of wooden huts: small shops, homes and a church on a steep hill overlooking the sea. The boy felt uncomfortable the church had been built so high. They could smell refuse and the scent of old cooking fires. Little kitchen gardens buffered some of the huts. There were raggedy-looking banana trees, their leaves dried the colour of brown paper bags. Half-naked children waved and shouted at them.

They saw an old, bent woman walking at the side of the road. She seemed a hundred years old and plodded along with the patience of a turtle. To the boy she looked like one: her neck stretched forward horizontally from her humped back, as she paused to look at them drive by, her eyes regarding them as if from another time.

A minute later, they passed a man bathing in his underwear at a standpipe on the side of the road. The man hissed at his mother; she ignored him.

"Where are we going?" the boy asked.

She hesitated, noting the fuel indicator, which registered almost full. "It's all right. Just a drive along the north coast, then we'll head back home and I'll go see Dad."

"Oh." He was unsure about it all, and his head hung low until they were beyond the village, heading to the most scenic part of the island.

An hour ago the boy was at home with his mother, and she had been on the telephone to his father. The door to his parents' bedroom had been shut, but he was able to hear his mother's voice. He knew they were quarrelling. After half an hour she came out of the bedroom and suggested they go for a drive; she needed to get out of the house: she had been trapped inside it for days, wondering; waiting.

The road, black in the bright light, is undulating. When the car speeds up, his mother's loose skirt, with patterns of red flowers, billows around her thighs. It's as if the boy and his mother, rising and falling with the car, are flying low along the island's coast. Her wedding ring, a single diamond set in gold, catches the sunlight when she adjusts her skirt or changes gears. They have passed no other cars for twenty minutes and seen no signs of human habitation for longer.

"Isn't it beautiful?" she says. "Carib Amerindians used to fish here. A long time ago."

"I suppose." He looks ahead at the open road, trying to avoid the dance of her skirt. But he wonders what her pale, firm thighs feel like; their texture and colour remind him of the long stretches of beaches they have passed, are passing. He imagines tucking her skirt back and resting his hand on her left leg, which is parted from the other toward him. He blushes at the thought. The wind picks up.

"Oh, is that all?" There is a slight edge of irritation in her voice. Her large, beautiful eyes are dark, tired.

"It's so clean and bright," he says. He pauses, deciding if she's encouraging him or demanding a response. Then: "Smooth, like skin. And sometimes I feel like we're flying." He does not look at her legs.

She meets his eyes, smiles. "That's nice." The edge to her voice has eased. "After the rainy season, there're always these deep colours. Except for the arid land here."

"We came here last year, didn't we?"

"Yes, that's right. Dad was with us. We collected pebbles for the garden, and you wrote about it for English Composition. 'A Day by the Seaside'. Remember?"

He frowns and looks away from the road, out to sea. His mother sees this and says, "We can stop higher up at a beach, if you like. Get some pebbles." She opens her handbag and takes out a packet of cigarettes and silver lighter. She rests them on her lap.

The car rises, near the edge of a cliff. The rocks are dark along the beaches, watery lustre surrounds them, and white caps flash on the sea. On the horizon the outline of another island is just visible. A vulture glides across the view, gains altitude in the breeze, then heads inland. The road continues, rising and falling, heading, it seems, to somewhere far away in the sky.

"There's a gas station up ahead, with a phone, if I remember. I'm going to call Dad."

He hits the door with his knee.

"What's the matter?"

"You and Dad are arguing again."

"No. I just need to chat with him." The irritation has returned to her voice. "That's all."

"It's an argument."

"Nonsense. I've to let him know we'll be a little late coming home. It's not safe to be out here for so long. He'll worry."

They descend to where the road is almost level with the sea. The breeze, gusty here, brings a strong scent of salt into the car. His hair ruffles.

She asks, "How's Troy?"

"He's gone away for the weekend, with his parents and sister."

"Well, Monday's a public holiday. You'll see him then. Maybe Dad will take you both to a movie."

"I don't think Dad will want to," he says with the finality of tone he has learned from his father.

Her shoulders and angular face slump, as if the fatigue from her eyes has spread there. They slow down, approaching the gas station. The road goes on, hilly scrubland on one side stretching to the low brown hills, and on the other, lifting above the sea and heading toward the sky.

The gas station office is a white, block-shaped building, its roof extending to shade two pumps. His mother parks so the pumps are between the car and the office. The interior of the office is visible when their eyes adjust to the shade. There is a single garage attached to the office, in which a tall man with long, rope-like hair is spraying water beneath an elevated car. Water blows out into the sunlight, creating rainbows. In the office, another man, with short hair, sits at a desk, rolling a pencil in the fingers of his right hand. He stares indifferently at the boy and his mother.

Before switching off the car engine, his mother looks around, making minimal eye contact with the two men. She gets out. The boy can hear the water in the garage; even smell its oily, sun-rich vapours. The men pay her no attention; they seem aware that she wants only to use the telephone. They look bored, tired.

His mother says, "I'll be about ten minutes. Wait here." She shuts her door.

He's not listening, not even seeing her; he's watching the man in the office, who continues playing with the pencil.

She is already walking to the telephone booth, which is near the garage. The boy watches her now. The man in the garage watches her too. As she approaches the telephone booth, the sea breeze blows her skirt up, showing the full length of the back of her legs and above, upper thighs pale and smooth, the texture and colour of a beach seen from high above the earth. Her underwear, black and narrow between her buttocks, flashes in the sunlight before her arm, long and slender, sweeps around and catches her skirt.

The boy sees the man in the garage grin and shake his head; then he looks at the other man in the office and sees the pencil freeze in his hand. His mother enters the telephone booth and lights a cigarette, dials a number; now and then she half-turns and pulls on her cigarette, revealing hollows in her cheeks. She holds the smoke in a moment, exhales forcefully, her head angling upwards, her eyes closing. After several minutes she opens the door of the booth and drops the cigarette. She steps on it and shuts herself back in. Her left arm folded across her chest, she repeatedly opens and closes the hinged top of the cigarette lighter with her thumb.

There is a battered No Smoking sign near the exit of the gas station. The boy sees it for the first time, sees the road going away from everything around him, and remembers his mother's promise about the pebbles. He glances at her and leaves the car, begins walking toward the beach. It is behind the office and down the hill. He passes white containers of ice, sees the man in the office smile and wave. The boy waves back. He likes the heat, breeze and ice cream advertisements painted on the office wall. Here the shadows are lengthening. The texture of sea and land is changing, promising the softer, deeper colours of late afternoon. The lower half of the wall, under the advertisements, is smeared in grease and oil. At the end of the wall a pipe is dripping, its puddle of water earthy-fresh in the salty air. He sees the two blues of horizon, sky and sea meeting in a perfect crease where one changes into the other, and he walks on, his eyes wide open and bright. At the top of a hill bristly with grass, he takes off his slippers, leaves them there, and goes down to the beach.

Unable to bear the hot sand, he runs down the last of the hill and out on to the vanishing sheen he saw earlier along the coast. The waves are gentle, sounding the word hush, drawing it out again and again.

He continues running, runs until tired, and then begins collecting pebbles whose shapes and colours interest him. When he has a handful, he lifts the end of his jersey, puts them in, and wraps them securely. The sun is behind him.

There is a long stick ahead where the tide slides back, its movement slow and casual. Froth rides the thin clear water and quivers in the wind. Another wave jumps abruptly when it meets the receding swash. He takes off his jersey, with the pebbles clicking pleasantly and still bagged, and rests it on the sand. The warmth of the sun is a nice sting on his back and shoulders. He picks up the stick and begins to draw a long line in the sand; soon he throws it, trying to hit a dry coconut thirty feet away. He misses, gets the stick, and begins to draw a long line in the sand again. The line takes form, becomes the elegant curves of a feminine figure. Her legs are much longer than her torso, and her head flows into long, thick hair. Then he draws a smaller figure, with short hair.

The stick is drying fast and he holds it at the sharper end. After picking up the pebbles, he walks off. The gas station is now only detectable from the glint of sunlight on its corrugated-iron roof.

Further on there is haze in front of a cliff right-angled from the coastal road. It is the largest concentration of afternoon sunlight, a tremendous curtain of tiny silver particles. It towers above the cliff's rocky base, and then disappears into the sky. As he heads toward it, he drags the stick behind him, making a long curving mark, like the lines of the woman left drawn in the sand.

He's in the haze, happy in the light. The wet rocks are dark and glinting. He throws the spear at them; it breaks in two and falls into the bright surf. Among the rocks there is one with a smooth, triangular slate surface angling at him. He finds a quartz-crystal stone and begins writing the words: *I am the first person here.* And indeed it appears so: he can see no sign of litter, nothing remotely connected to human beings except the gas station's roof, a swathe of bright silver from this distance. The sun will soon sink behind the gas station, and sea and sky will turn a darker blue. He turns and walks up the beach, unwraps his jersey and lets the pebbles fall. He selects one, dusts it, and studies it closely. He likes those with spots like freckles best; when he has cleaned and looked at them all, the ones he prefers – some because of shape, too – he puts aside. The others he gathers up and pelts into the sea as far as he can, hurting himself with the effort. He looks at those he has kept, decides he needs to find more for his mother. She always enjoys collecting buckets of pebbles and arranging them in her garden. He knows she will love these he has now.

Through the sound of the sea he hears a shout. He sees a tall figure waving its arms in the distance and running to him. He picks up his jersey, shakes the sand off, and rewraps the pebbles. By the time he is finished, the figure is clear: it is the man who was cleaning the car at the gas station.

"Ay!" the man yells. He is wet and wearing only underwear. His hair, much more than earlier, is like pieces of rope.

"Ay!" the man repeats.

The boy clutches the wrapped pebbles to his chest.

"What you doing here for so long?" the man asks. His left hand is a fist. "You don't know your mother want you, or what? I hope she beat you good! If you was my child, I beat you till you bawl like cut pig. Is what you doing here?"

The boy doesn't answer. The man leaps forward, close to him, his feet digging into the sand. He staggers back to regain his balance and the boy looks up at his red, violent eyes.

"You want me to lash you?" The man raises his hand swiftly and the boy ducks, legs trembling, his shoulders hunching up around his ears. He feels a hand snatch at his shoulder and his knees give out. The man pulls him to his feet and shakes him.

"What you got in that cloth, boy?" The man yanks the jersey and the pebbles drop to the sand, clicking against each other. He starts to laugh.

"Is what you have there? Like you want a beach to carry home, or what?"

"They're for my mother," the boy says with great effort. Then he begins to cry. He reaches for the pebbles in front of him, begins picking them up, putting them back into the folds of his jersey. The man, hands on his hips, is backing off drunkenly, looking at the sky, his body beginning to sway, the knees bending for rhythm, his laughter changing to singing. The words are unclear.

The boy starts running as fast as he can. Behind him, the man curses and a moment later a silver cigarette lighter skitters along the firm sand beside the boy. But he looks straight ahead, sees only the gas station with its corrugated-iron roof of silver.

He tries to trudge up the hill, slips halfway; scrambles the rest, holding the wrapped jersey of pebbles and breathing heavily. He doesn't remember his slippers, but they are gone. At the top he looks at the route he has run. The man is nowhere. His mother's car is still there, the back fender protruding beyond one of the gas pumps. He walks toward it, but stops before he passes the display of advertisements on the wall. Turns back to the pipe, hesitates, wipes the tears from his face, and then goes to it, stoops, and starts washing the pebbles, his face. It seems the only sensible thing to do.

"Get in the car – immediately."

He spins around. She is there, glaring at him, her arms folded.

"I got some pretty pebbles for the garden." He has tried to say this with confidence. He does not look at her.

"I said, *Get* in the car."

He puts the cleaned pebbles back in the jersey and goes to the car, unable to look at his mother. She follows him, and as he gets into the car, he sees the man in the office. His feet are on the desk. He is eating a sandwich with slow relish and ignores the boy, who looks away and shuts the car door.

His mother opens her door and enters the car slowly, wincing. Then she drives out of the gas station, continues on in the direction they were heading an hour ago. They road begins to rise. In the distance it's possible to see a large bay, still azure in the failing light, curving on both sides, its blue edges a definite border, separating the low brown hills.

The afternoon is ending and the sun's rays set off the interior of the car.

When she shifts gears, he notices her diamond ring is missing. And then he begins to see things he does not want to consider or understand. There is a bruise on her wrist, purpling, lifting. He smells blood, but does not know where it's coming from, or even what it is, not quite yet. He looks out of the window at the sea, at the blue end of the earth. Then he looks at his mother again. He sees more this time. Red-fresh bruises on her shins, a tear on her dress above the knees, scratches on her neck, darkening bruises along her forearms and elbows.

He wants to be far away from everything human. Something terrible has happened, is going to happen. He knows it with the same certainty he knows the amber and orange sky is there above an ocean whose weight now rests in his heart, his eyes, and brain. He makes an effort to sit up, to resist the feeling of suffocation, of something being quenched forever in him.

He must stare out of the window.

There, on the sea, in the deepening light, a huge sense of time, larger than ever before, attends him.

And then it comes.

His mother stamps the brake. The car swerves and screeches to a halt in the middle of the road, its front pointing to the scrubland on their right. The pebbles fall to his feet, clicking against each other, a reminder, almost welcome at first, that an hour ago a better life was elsewhere.

"Why did you leave the car? *What* gave you the right? *Who* told you to leave?"

She is hitting him about the face and head, clenching her hands into fists and pummelling his neck and head with all her furious strength, bashing his ears. The blows, after what seems like a while, are no longer painful. He's most aware of the sound of her fists on his body; it's as if he has already left himself.

"Never leave the car like that! Never!" Her voice has risen to a scream. "Never ever leave me like that! Never leave me!"

She keeps beating him.

It occurs to him, dazed and numb, to get out of the car.

He gets out of the car.

She falls across his seat, sobbing, fists relaxing; reaches for him. She tries to speak, but can't.

Arms about his head, pain now burning in his ears, on his face and neck, he goes to the side of the road. He turns and watches her. She pulls herself halfway out of his door and begins coughing and choking. Within seconds she vomits onto the road.

He is moving off, he is leaving her, walking along the road, then running, determined never to look back, never to slow down, certain that if he keeps moving fast enough, he will never stop.

THE MARCHES OF BLUE

Nicolas arrived on the island in early summer, after his third year at university in Boston, with plans to begin writing a novel or history about his family. He'd lugged along twenty books for ideas and guidance; they took up half his bed, and each night he fell asleep to their voices.

The mass of Caribbean Sea and its sky were rich blues, the colours he loved most. The island was dry, its green fading, and there was heat to contend with, something that could be relentless even when breezes rustled trees on the island's northeast coast. This was where Nicolas's grandmother lived, a tall, sturdy seventy-five year-old with neat grey hair, with her dog Tina, otherwise alone. Her villa overlooked bright, green-blue bays, coves and smaller islands with names like Manacles Reef, Hell's Gate, Little Man of War Island, and Exchange Bay. Now on moonless nights smugglers used the dark bulks of the islands and coves to conduct their business. Nicolas imagined their boats sliding across the black water toward them, engines softly puttering. Once, late at night, he heard a gunshot.

At breakfast, his grandmother said, "I'll drop you to the beach after lunch, if you like; on my way into town. There's some shopping I must do today."

Nicolas looked at the mahogany furniture in the living room, the low stonewall porch outside, then the garden with soft fine grass, greener close to the shade of the house. Cacti, red and purple bougainvillea and small citrus trees were all arranged with the attentive eye of a landscape artist in the dry earth beyond the grass. Since independence, according to his grandmother, the island had lost any real sense of discipline and responsibility, and she was determined that these qualities should be visible on her property. Her several acres had been fenced to keep the bush out. In the dry weather she had the gardener work regularly. A cistern under the house collected rain from the roof, but in these dry times anything growing beyond the house's thirty-foot perimeter was left to fend for itself.

"I'd like that," he said.

In the mid-afternoon Nicolas usually walked down to the small cove below the house where his grandfather first took him years ago to swim. Like the rest of the land around his grandmother's property it was uninhabited and inviting. But Nicolas also loved to see other parts of the island whenever he could; sometimes he took a bus or hitched a ride.

Later, from the porch, he looked at the sea and small islands and thought of the coming hours at Beggar's Bay, where, with the exception of a few tourists, he would have the beach to himself. Wind made a sound like rain through the dry trees beneath his grandmother's property. He looked at the dying leaves and then up and over them at the neat line of morning horizon. It was a place where you could be drawn to imagine what was happening out of sight. In school between the ages of seven and nine he had sketched men and women on an island, separated by hills of trees and curves of green coast, or hidden away in yachts behind bluffs and peninsulas. Often there were scuba divers in the drawings, people at peace in the silent, dense blue of sea.

When Nicolas was ten he wanted to be a painter, and one day devoted an entire afternoon to the shape and colours of a glider in a sea-blue sky, oil on canvas, which his mother had bought for him. The previous year an award had been given him for a watercolour of a stout man walking through a storm of red raindrops, umbrella and trees bending in the wind, but the glider in the sky was a failure. He wrecked the canvas. Soon he was trying to read serious books, and though his ability to make readable sentences and paragraphs was minimal, he'd decided by the time he was twelve to be a writer. Everyone but his grandfather had found it amusing. To his grandmother and parents his announcement had been a joke.

There were whitecaps on the sea: pillows of cotton drifting in. Bright, green water surrounded the small islands. Africa, Nicolas knew, was somewhere over there, far away to the east. His grandfather had told him that. A yacht, like a white arrowhead in the distance, passed behind one of the islands. Keeping very still, Nicolas could detect its movement. He felt cool breeze, the sun's heat, and there were scents of earth and sea, iron and salt, and the light rot of vegetation from the land below.

His grandmother called him.

"In a minute."

"I want you here. Now."

The glazed terra-cotta tiles beneath his bare feet were delightfully cool as he went to locate her. In the dining room, he glanced at his grandfather's cabinet of books. His grandmother disliked anyone reading them; they were not to be removed, only admired through the glass, kept crystal bright by Ethlin, who came three times a week from a nearby village. Since his grandfather's death he'd managed to read four; and on this trip, three days after his arrival, he'd woken at three in the morning to remove another: *The Marches of El Dorado* by Michael Swan.

Nicolas's grandfather had been retired a year from his position as chairman of several companies in the region, and was pursuing other interests – poetry, carpentry and farming – when he died. He had worked hard all his life, starting in his father's shop in British Guiana, at the age of eleven. He had taught himself mathematics and accounts while his first two children played around his legs under the kitchen table. He had paid for this house to be built, had helped the workmen with a sense of joy they found peculiar in a white man.

Nicolas wrote the scene in his mind.

Boss, come go take a relax. We soon finish.

Cedar, my grandfather said, sliding his palm along the smooth length of a fat plank. I love the smell. Take your time… There're beers in the fridge for later. His expression was of a man savouring the fact he'd finally found time to do what he wanted most in his life: smile just lifting the corners of his mouth, and blue eyes soft, appreciating the task at hand, the simple, physical pleasure of it. Shirtless, and still in the socks and brown dress shoes he wore to work, with his balding head of grey-brown hair tufting at the sides, an occasional strand lifting upward in the breeze, and belted khaki shorts falling to just above his knees, he looked like an unkempt lord. I later gathered a handful of cedar shavings – a curly mass of blonde, springy Rasta locks – and stuffed my nose into it, breathing deeply.

The workmen accepted my grandfather with tacit respect, seeming to think he was an old man just playing young. Thirteen years old at the time, I heard the offer of beer through the window of the master bedroom, where my grandmother sat knitting on her bed, her back up against the headboard, separated from my grandfather's bed by an antique desk. Every day after lunch she was to be found knitting there, her head bent as if in prayer. I had gone in to give her the glass of water she had sent for. The maid usually left right before we had the lunch she'd prepared, so I was often told to do things in the afternoons. Hearing my grandfather's words, she'd sighed and said, Honestly, God give me strength. Beer. He's going to give them beer.

Nicolas knew there was much more to his family history than such anecdotes, but his grandmother, the only person alive who knew what he didn't, was reluctant to tell the stories.

Nicolas heard her walking on the gravel driveway. Then his name again, louder, so he quickened his pace, remembering it was her house and food, that he was still being supported by her at university. His parents, who both lived in Barbados and whom he'd not seen in eighteen months, were divorcing, and the cost of the lawyer's fees and settlement had been too much for his father.

His grandmother, sitting half in the sun, had Tina by her collar. The dog had mange. "Keep still, Tina. Look – bring me that bowl on the car. Be quick about it."

Nicolas saw a yellowy cloud in the bowl of water. "Let me stir it first."

"I should think so, and put a little more medicine in. There's a spoon there. One teaspoonful."

The dog whimpered. "Oh, keep quiet, Tina," she said.

As Nicolas came over with the solution, Tina watched him with wide brown eyes. She whimpered again. He put the bowl down and sat on the garage floor. His grandmother dipped a cup in the medicine, poured some on Tina's back, and began rubbing the solution in. Tina continued to whine. Nicolas clicked his tongue a couple times and Tina relaxed, began panting, sitting quite still and gazing out across the driveway at some potted crotons and pink zinnias. His grandmother continued to pour the solution, rubbing Tina's back with increasing concern.

"Want me to take over?"

"No. Bring some water for her. Notice how much she's enjoying it now she knows there's no pain? Life's a holiday, eh Tina?" Tina whined and made to move away, but his grandmother grabbed her by the scruff of her neck and yanked her closer.

His grandmother looked at him. "Water?"

He rose, found the bowl, and went to the kitchen.

"Don't waste any," she called after him. "Remember, this is a dry island." Then she recited the note she'd once taped up in all the bathrooms years ago.

"If it's yellow, let it mellow; if it's brown, flush it down."

At the sink, filling Tina's bowl, he looked through the varnished louvres and saw, in the distance, a village on a green rise near where he would soon be going. The sky was cloudless as usual. There was nothing but low rolling hills of fading green, like the moors of England, and too few trees between him and the distant village. Many years ago there had been lush forests on the island.

He went back into the garage. His grandmother, drying her hands on a kitchen cloth, was looking at the circular flower-bed in the middle of the driveway. She shook her head. The hibiscuses, shaded by a young flamboyant, were dying.

"I am going to have to do something about George. If this is what he calls gardening, he has another thought coming."

Nicolas said nothing. Tina whined. He helped his grandmother with some other chores (trimming a jasmine vine in the house's main entrance, moving potted plants out of the sun), then read for the rest of the morning in his room, hearing wind in the dry trees and feeling the immense presence of the blue sea.

After lunch they drove down the stony hill, passing a dry swamp on the left. Wind in the long feathery grass around the swamp made the movements of some huge, invisible creature. Dust rose from between the swamp and the road and blew toward the car. With the windows wound up, they heard only the crunch of the tires on the road. The air-conditioner blew cold air on Nicolas's thighs.

They saw the gardener, George, walking along the dirt road, a plastic bag dangling from his right hand. Nicolas's grandmother stopped the car, lowered her window, and spoke to George. Elderly and tall, he nodded and said yes to her every request and demand, sweating, standing at a respectable distance, his body slightly bent, backing away and then stepping forward again.

"Yes Misuss," he said again. "I understand."

When she'd finished telling him about the condition of the flowers in the driveway, where to get extra water for them, how much to use, and that he would have to get another job if he couldn't follow her simple directions, George greeted Nicolas, smiling and nodding a little. Nicolas did the same. He'd met the gardener on his last visit a year ago, when his grandmother had first hired him. George was losing his teeth. His eyes were red and wet.

"I'll be back in a couple of hours," Nicolas's grandmother said.

George bowed a little.

They went on up a potholed unpaved road, turning sharply to the left, then to the right, before coming to several primary-coloured wooden houses. They were small dwellings, no more than two or three rooms. To their right, the land, covered in thorny bushes, sloped downwards. At the bottom were middle-class houses near inlets lined in mangrove. There, narrowing in among abandoned fishing boats rotting away on land hacked up to mark possession, the sea lost its grandeur.

"We can wind down the windows now," his grandmother said. "I wish to God that road could be paved." She switched off the air-conditioner.

Ahead of them, waiting at the side of the road and gripping a bulging red bag, was a heavy-set woman.

"I should stop for Albertine."

They slowed, and though other traffic was unlikely at this hour, his grandmother pulled in quite close to the side of the road. Albertine waved at them.

"Mornin' Mrs. Roberts."

"Hullo Albertine. How are you?"

23

"Oh, I is fine-fine. And yuhself?"

"Not too bad. Where are you going?"

"Nicolas! Is you!" She reached her hand in and patted his arm.

"Where are you going, Albertine?"

"The church, thank you very much, Mrs. Roberts. I meeting my sister there to catch the bus to town. Eh-eh, but look how grownup Nicolas get! Last time I see you was at your grandfather funeral, outside the church, not so?"

Nicolas nodded.

He leaned back and opened the door. Albertine put the bag in with effort, near the opposite door, and then let herself onto the seat, in the middle. The car sank. She was dressed in a splash of bright colours and smelled lightly of bath soap. As she shut the door, she laughed hesitantly, shifting and twisting into a comfortable position.

"So, how long you here for, Nicolas? Eh, but you looking so like a man now. Before you was thin like a boy. Now you eating like man!"

"Eats like a horse, if you ask me; even things he shouldn't," his grandmother said. "He's here on holiday, but hoping to do some work."

"And what work you hoping to do, Nicolas?"

"Some writing."

He could see Albertine in the rear-view mirror; sometimes he turned to her.

"So you going to be a writer! Very good. Maybe you will write some calypso?" Albertine laughed again.

"The writing's just a hobby," his grandmother said. "He should be starting his Master's degree in business next year September –"

"But it good to have a hobby, something to relax with. And it better if he could make a living writing book. Everybody nowadays only want they children to be doctor, businessman or lawyer. Is only money feeding they eye – and lawyers here too *wicked*. So much of them wrap up in that drug business with the government and selling land for the hotels and tourism to all them world-class crook."

She said these last two sentences with contempt, but quietly.

His grandmother looked ahead.

"Yes," Nicolas said, agreeing with Albertine.

His grandmother cleared her throat.

"The weather *dry* this year, Mrs. Roberts! How the garden doing?"

Nicolas glanced at Albertine in the rear-view mirror: she was smiling, her fat cheeks pushing her eyes up into mischievous slits.

"God, yes," his grandmother said. "I had some young crotons Mr. Solomon gave me. I replanted them five times. No amount of water and fertilizer would help them. Eventually they just died. That's that, I said."

"George couldn't save them, Mrs. Roberts?"

"*George?*"

Albertine said nothing. Nicolas looked out of the window.

His grandmother accelerated until they were travelling at fifty-five miles an hour on the narrow road. The car dipped into a depression and rose. Her leather-bound notebook, in the depression of the dashboard, danced up, fell off and landed at her sandalled feet. Air whipped through the windows and ruffled Nicolas's dark brown hair. He thought the sound of the tyres on the concrete road was like the hiss, magnified a hundred times, of bare limbs moving on sheets. They were passing another village, the grey wooden shacks flashing by like faded watercolours. He bent down to get the notebook and she knocked his hand away with her leg, a sudden movement that caused him to blush.

"I'll get it later," she said.

He glanced at Albertine, but she was looking out of the window, eyes half-closed, allowing the wind to flail her face.

"How's Cuthbert, Albertine?"

"Oh, he's fine, Mrs. Roberts. Still with the rum a little, but I watches him. That rum and this sun don't mix."

His grandmother mumbled something about mad dogs, Englishmen and the midday sun; then said, "How right you are, Albertine."

"Nicolas does have a little?" Albertine asked with a wheezy giggle.

"Not me, I stick to beer now. Much less hard on you."

"That's good. I allows myself a little beer, too. A little is good.

But West Indies people could *drink*, eh Mrs. Roberts! Since from small. All of them."

"Everything in moderation, I say. You can't appreciate it otherwise. How people can go to parties every weekend and get silly on alcohol is beyond me."

Nicolas said, "But can they change? Sometimes I think they drink because they see little chance of a future. Or maybe there's not much else to do."

"Is true, Nicolas. They ain't want to change, yes. Change for what? Change how? Too much freedom, but only to do nothing. The government, now, them do whatever them want, so much that poor people can't do anything except survive. And drink rum."

His grandmother said, "Doing what you want isn't necessarily the best thing for you." She looked at him, her face set: an expression of resistance if ever he'd seen one.

The car began slowing.

Ahead, goats were crossing. There were ten, some of them trailing ropes and bleating, oblivious to the car. Two stopped in the middle of the road and began chewing grass in between cracks in the grey concrete. His grandmother blew the horn. The goats raised their heads and stared, their eyes like boiled eggs, stupid and comical looking. The bigger of the two pointed his horns at the car and shook his head. A smooth, slim-limbed boy, clad in dark underwear, pranced out of the bush on the left and chased the goats off. He grinned enthusiastically at Nicolas's grandmother, came over to her window, put out his hand, and said, "A dollar, Misuss! A dollar!" Then he recognized Nicolas and waved.

"Isn't that Benny?" Nicolas asked.

"Yes," Albertine said. "Miss Dorothy boy." Her voice was low.

His grandmother managed to smile and shake her head at Benny, but before she could drive on, he sprang in front of the car and elegantly cart-wheeled across the road to join the goats.

"Those *silly* goats. The other day Mrs. Solomon told me she nearly hit one on her way back from church. She hit the brakes so hard, she said, a tyre burst. It shouldn't be allowed."

"Yes," Albertine said. "They's troublesome to the drivers sometimes."

In the rear-view mirror Albertine looked sad.

They arrived at the block-shaped church, with its pitched wooden roof and grey stone walls stained with sun-dried fungus. Palm trees, bent and tired-looking, swayed their flickering, sun-tinted leaves like large scissors. An old man with patchy grey hair was sitting on a box near the entrance to the church. He sat hunched forward, gripping a stick for support. He wore a raggedy black suit which might have been in style in the 1930s, and stared at Nicolas's grandmother. The left side of his face jumped involuntarily and his lips were collapsed in a toothless mouth; he moved them constantly, as if tasting the soft flesh. He mumbled something and then spat on the ground near his box.

"All right, Albertine, take care," his grandmother said, in an indifferent voice. She never looked at the old man.

"Okay, Mrs. Roberts. Thank you very much. You take care now." She leaned forward. "You must write a nice book, Nicolas."

"I'll try," he said, twisting around and looking straight at Albertine's eyes.

"Don't take too much sun. This heat too bad!" And pulling her red bag after her, she laughed with effort and got out.

Nicolas saw Albertine go straight to the old man sitting on the box.

Several minutes later, after passing up through the village he had seen from the house earlier, they came to a road winding through a small plain. The land around them was flat and dry, so the detours in the road were redundant.

His grandmother said, "There were trees here once, so the winding was quite pleasant – shaded and cool. Then they cut them down, a few years into independence, to grow vegetables. It's such a dry island, for God's sake. It failed pretty quickly – no incentive for it to succeed; somebody had already made money off clearing the land, so now there's nothing except a winding road… But that's such a minor problem today, compared to the drug trade and politics… We should have remained a colony."

Nicolas said nothing.

A mile from the hotel, the road became smooth and straight with robust clumps of bougainvillea on either side. To their left, beyond the gardens, was the hotel's garbage dump, evident by the scent of food rot. Sprinklers, operating at full force, showered the bougainvillea and the fresh, neat grass lining the driveway.

His grandmother blocked her nose. "The hotels can't even be bothered with decent waste disposal," she said. "Yet what else is there for a small island like this to do?"

"Not much – so long as it's run a certain way."

"Now there you may have something, scribe." Her voice was still melancholy.

"I hope I do have something, there."

And then it came as clear as the day around them.

"Have you thought about your plans for next September? For the master's degree?"

He shook his head.

"I'll pay for some kind of business degree, nothing else: no literature, creative writing, journalism, or whatever. Your grand-father had the same idea, once. Imagine – he wanted to leave his job and write. Teach for a living. Your father had just been born. Imagine the step down we would've had to take. I nearly left him."

She stopped the car under the trees near the small hotel at the end of the beach. The sea was still, keen blue; the sand so bright at first it hurt his eyes to look at it. The sky, pure blue, made the whole seascape seem alive with the mystery he'd sensed in his drawings as a child. He'd felt completely free, at ease with his imagination, in his drawings, if they went well. He sensed that experience beginning now. After drawing his seascapes, he'd often felt something else in the picture, beyond the objects and people within it, which he could not see, but knew was there: another story happening just over a hill, perhaps.

"What time shall I come for you?" she asked.

When he was about to gesture whatever time she found convenient, she laughed – a brief release of air – as if disdainfully appraising him while the conversation about the island and his lack of plans continued in her head.

"Five, five-thirty?" he said.

She bent down and picked up her leather-bound notebook near her feet, with noticeable effort. "Five-thirty, then."

"Great." He got out.

"Aren't you forgetting a few things?"

She pointed at his beach bag. The cover of her leather-bound notebook flipped open in a gust of sea breeze, and he saw the shopping list for the week, set line by line, as were payments and appointments.

"Careful of any odd strangers on the beach."

"You mean the tourists?"

"Yes, those people who live such free, hedonistic lives. For a while." She drove off.

He walked onto the empty beach, determined to enjoy his time. Another small hotel was at its other end, against a rise of rocks. Stunted vegetation lay on the rocks, and some trees struggled for the earth between them, extending dry and twisted branches.

Midway down the beach, Nicolas spread his towel, sat, and took off his shirt. He tugged his swim trunks up his thighs, removed a book from his bag, and began reading. He soon lost concentration, his senses responding to the soporific rustling of the trees, the blank-white sand, clean and open as empty pages, water slipping gently on the shore, light wind against his skin – and that ever-present, eternal blue above, beyond and behind him. The words in their neat even-sided arrangement, the shape of letters with their varying formations began to blur. The words became queer, ink-black shapes, like long lines of people on a white desert landscape seen from high above. As he stared at the book in the bright sunlight and turned each sharp-edged page, the possibility of a paper cut occurred to him. Then even this interest palled and the book slipped from his hold and he stared out across the ocean.

"Where is Africa?"

His grandfather pointed to where the sea was darkest, to where clouds were gathering on the horizon. "Far, far over there."

The house was a few weeks from completion and they were standing on the point about two hundred yards from it, just above the cove where they would soon be going. The workmen were gone and his grandfather was sipping a beer.

"Want some?" His grandfather, shirtless, had been working with the carpenters. Dark and red moles were scattered on his upper chest.

Nicolas drank some beer and made a face.

*His grandfather smiled and said, "You'll learn in time to like it...
You'll learn soon enough."*

"Is it a storm?"

"Think so. Maybe a squall. It just needs to come a little closer."

"Why?"

"Colour."

"What?"

*His grandfather began walking down a path through the bush,
brambles catching at his arms, legs and scratching the skin bloody. He
ignored this and told Nicolas to come if he wanted to see something
beautiful.*

Nicolas got up and went into the water. Its piercing coolness
tensed him as he dove under into blue silence. He released air
lazily, let go snorkel and face mask, and sank with them to the
sand, which was paler here, as pale as the margins of his book. The
view ran out in front of him, so clear, like another kind of day.
Lying there, using up his air, he imagined he was inside the dense,
blue atmosphere of a planet similar to earth. His lungs began to
burn, but he did not rise; the sight before him, the submarine
quiet and weakened gravity, kept him there. He rose only when
blood pounded in his temples.

On the beach, near the hotel his grandmother had stopped at,
a young woman was watching him through a pair of binoculars.
With her knees drawn up to her chest, she appeared to be wearing
nothing. A spear gun lay next to her. When she lowered the
binoculars and stood, he saw their case slung on her shoulder, and
a green bikini bottom, riding high across her hips. As she passed
his things on the beach, looking down at them and putting the
binoculars into their case, her pace quickened. Her long legs,
muscles flexing as she strode along the shore, were very brown,
as brown as the rest of her, and peeling. She looked up as she
walked; black hair in a tight bun. One of her arms swung
sweepingly, while the other steadied the case. Her buttocks, a
firm, prominent undulation, appeared to balance the protrusions
of her breasts, which were smooth and swollen, tipped with dark
nipples and swaying.

She waved at him, and as he thought to return the greeting, she tripped one foot on the other, recovered without falling, and went on. Nicolas blushed for her and himself. She didn't look back. Where had she come from? He hadn't seen her arrive. She was just suddenly there. He kept watching her, and saw her enter the small hotel, against the rise of rocks, at the far end of the beach. He hoped she would reappear, but she didn't.

He walked over to where the woman had been, by a high coral-jagged cliff. Beneath it, away from its rocky base, was a reef. He slid in with his snorkel and mask and saw the reef was cut up this way and that with channels of sand, about four feet wide, winding and pearl-white; from above he imagined it would resemble an irregular jigsaw puzzle. Fish – dashes of silver and green – blended into the blue until he arrived at a mass of brain coral, where they were multicoloured – blue, red, yellow, green, orange – and smaller. Shades of blue and green surrounded him; deeper water, darker colours, the bay and ocean were to his left.

The blue depths lured him to swim over the brain coral, to float above a drop of twenty vertical feet of coral cliff. He saw pale sand below, sloping down and away into a huge silence of ever-deepening blue. He held onto the brain coral, looking down. His breath quickened through the snorkel. He gazed outward, gradually calming himself. Then he let go of the coral mass, filled his lungs, kicked his legs frog-fashion and, using his hands like fins and flaps, spiralled down. Silence became a clamp against his head, especially his ears; his body felt hugged over by water. At the bottom of the coral cliff, he released some air and stood gazing into the distance: pearl-white sand fading into a rich-blue blur: yet another, deeper kind of silence. He removed his swim trunks, held them in his left hand, leaned forward and, like a moon-walker, bounced once, twice, three times, and came to a path going upward, a division in the coral-and-rock cliff. A huge shadow of hundreds of diamond-and-triangular shapes moved along the cliff. He turned and saw a shoal of large fish receding elegantly into the blue. Startled, he backed up against the cliff and winced when his back made contact with its crustaceous growths. Moray eels lived in the recesses of such places – he stepped well away. Then he thought of sharks: there were no fish about now; something large was hunting.

A few seconds later he saw someone swimming at half depth, fifty feet away, gripping both handles of a dark spear gun. The person surfaced, then re-submerged, staying at a depth of about eight feet. Nicolas was about to get into his swim trunks when he noticed, peripherally, a play of light coming from above: the figure was thrashing – then stillness. At that moment he thought the gun was being pointed at him. He opened his mouth and jerked backwards, choking on water. His heart began to pound, his blood and lungs raged, desperate for air. He went straight up, forgetting his swim trunks, and swam on his back over the coral cliff, toward the sand paths, heaving and coughing great breaths and looking at the sky.

He rested in the shallows.

Across the water, not far from where he had surfaced, a dark-haired head showed and an arm grabbed off the face mask, splashing water. It was the young woman who'd been spying on him. She was gasping for air and looking about. When she saw him, she yelled, "Please, I'm so sorry to have frightened you! I have your bathing suit!" Her accent was French.

She began swimming on her back toward him, clutching the spear gun and face mask in one hand.

As she approached, he bent his legs until his nose was an inch above the water, tucked his genitals down between his thighs, and folded his arms on his hips. He hoped she was still topless so he would not feel too embarrassed.

He saw she was.

She said, "I was frightened out there – there was a shark. Did you see the fish? It was after them."

Nicolas didn't answer.

She handed him his swim trunks, and didn't turn away, so he did. He laughed, shook his head. "I didn't see a shark."

His trunks on, he faced her, blushing a little. She put a hand to her forehead and wiped her face. A long, blue-purple vein pulsed on the side of her neck; her face was flushed. Below her left ear, spiralling down to her shoulder, there was a blend of chocolate-brown freckles and a few tiny, protruding moles.

"Are you all right?" Nicolas asked.

"Oh yes."

Near where her breasts met her underarms, the skin and flesh were delicate, the colour aqueous. From the peeling on her arms and shoulders, on her left upper breast, she'd had too much sun.

They shook hands.

"Rickette."

"Nicolas."

Her smile – one front tooth was crooked – spread wide and sincere. Her dark brown skin defied definition. They swam back together.

They sat by his things on the beach. She hid her binoculars under her towel.

"I noticed your wave," he said after a while.

"Yes." She laughed and blushed. "Such strange weather today, breezy and hot." She was nervous, fidgeting with the sand.

"Yes," he said, not really thinking so. There were light clusters of freckles under her eyes. Her lustrous black hair was still pinned up at the back.

"Where are you staying?" Rickette asked.

"My grandmother's. North of here." He looked in that general direction. "Where are you from?"

"Martinique, I was born there, but now I am working in Paris for a long time. My mother came from here."

He liked her nervousness, part of a shyness he saw now. "What was her name?"

"Oh, it doesn't matter. She's been gone for a long time." Rickette looked at the ocean.

"The sun is not be trifled with," he said, indicating her peeling skin with a nod of his head. Saying the sentence, he'd known it was not one of his own – his grandfather's – and he began to see Rickette and himself as if from beyond, as if secretly observing her and a young man. Why was this happening? It had happened before – always when he'd felt a thrill at being alive in a particular moment and situation.

"What do you do?" he asked.

"I teach high school in Paris. Geography, history, English."

She drew her knees to her chest and hugged them, her breasts pressing in against her thighs. She tucked some loose hair behind her right ear. "Will you be here tomorrow?"

"I'd like to."

"We can explore the reef together, if you like."

"Wonderful," he said.

It was cooler. She undid her damp hair and let it fall down her back and around her breasts. She picked up the spear gun and they both stood. "I'll go now."

"Tomorrow, then."

"Absolutely," she said. Walking off, she looked back at him over her brown shoulder, smiled again and said, "Take care."

The late afternoon light was soft, the colour of ripening mangoes.

Fifteen minutes later, at five-thirty precisely, his grandmother blew the car horn from amongst the trees.

On the road leading away from the hotel's driveway, dust billowing behind the car, his grandmother asked, "Well, how was it?" She was in slacks and a peach-coloured shirt, neat, looking straight ahead at the road.

"Good. I love snorkelling. I think I'll come by bus tomorrow afternoon. After lunch."

"No, I'll drop you."

"I can manage. It'll save you trouble. Riding the bus should give me something interesting to write about."

"I doubt it."

"How was your afternoon?" he asked.

"Oh, fine. Except I had to fire George."

Nicolas looked at her.

"George," she said. "You remember him."

"Yes. But I really didn't think you'd let him go."

"He was doing his own thing in the garden; neglecting this and that, being attentive to the wrong things. He never listened. Like your grandfather. Do you understand?"

"Think so."

"You do?" she asked, with a sudden glance. "Good."

The fading green land around the village had darkened. The dusty road was the colour of ash, and would soon be bright, almost incandescent, when the moon and stars lit the sky. Between the low hills the sun sat on the horizon like a fat, orange penny. He thought of Rickette, of how they had met. As they passed through Wilikies, its name suggested a certain island romance, and his afternoon something a would-be tourist in Boston or New York City, flipping through brochures about far away tropical places, might envision.

Near the church, its rough stonewall in detailed relief in the setting sun, they saw Benny herding goats back across the road.

"Not again." His grandmother sighed. "Somehow he always seems to know when I'm about to pass here." She tapped the steering wheel with the fingers of her left hand, smallest first, others following in an orderly fashion, repeating this again and again until the fullest gesture of impatience possible with her hand had been expressed.

The goats seemed to have multiplied and were wandering around in the middle of the road. Benny was taking his time, coming toward the car, grinning. Soon he was upon them, begging. His grandmother looked away. Benny's face became serious. Nicolas felt in his bag for cash, but his grandmother, never to be outfaced, began beeping her way through the herd. A few of the animals threatened the car with their horns, bluffing. The car went on, carefully, slowly. Ahead, the road rose with no end in sight to the rich-blue evening sky. Behind them came Benny's voice: "A dollar, white lady! Ten thousand dollars! Is *my* father money!"

Black night, black time: Nicolas was on the roof of the house, sipping a beer and sitting in an aluminium recliner. All through dinner at the kitchen table with his grandmother, he'd heard Tina whining outside for him. They had made small talk, but when he'd tried to ask her about Benny's shouted words, she'd given him a look so severe he'd said nothing more until after dessert, when he'd excused himself and said he was going to sit on the roof and watch the stars.

In the night there was wind, fragrant with moisture and sea salt: the scent of his grandfather, still ignoring the thorny brambles, half-naked and smelling of fresh sweat and iron, as they walked down the path to the sea. Nicolas wanted to see something beautiful. The stones on the path, edgy bits of glittering quartz and coral, almost punctured his shoes.

Nicolas wished there was a boat hidden somewhere below and they were going to escape from his grandmother, go to Africa and have adventures.

"How long would it take us to go to Africa?"

"Sailing?"

"Yes, a sailboat," the boy said, glad, as always, his grandfather was taking him seriously.

"As long as it took the storm. A couple weeks, maybe more, depending on wind."

He watched his grandfather's sure footing and tried to copy it, slipped and fell, cutting his knee on the stones. In the approaching storm's dull light, Nicolas's blood was closer in colour to black than red. His grandfather laughed gently, helping him up. "Walk at your own pace," he said. "Don't copy me. Don't be anything but yourself."

"Right."

The storm was rising on the faraway horizon, tinting the blues and greens of sea, darkening the east, soothing his retinae. The man and boy came upon a pebbly, sandy beach, no more than twenty yards long, a little cove where, apart from smugglers, no one but his grandfather went. There were several jagged rocks, like the remains of an ancient citadel, reaching out in a broken embrace toward the sea's east. The wind began to gust and water flopped and slapped on the beach. Behind them, near the path, stood a large triangular rock, taller than Nicolas. His grandfather looked at it, his face solemn for a moment, then at Nicolas. He smiled.

"We're going swimming, boy. Come on." His grandfather removed his shoes and socks and stripped, revealing a slack-skinned but fit body. There was grey hair on his shoulders, his chest and down to his stomach. He waded into the water, dove under and surfaced beyond the rocks. Nicolas, embarrassed, undressed to his underwear and dashed into the water, tasting the first rain of the storm. He saw his grandfather swimming towards a low island, one of many along the coast. Lightning started, blue-white cracks in space and time, and Nicolas sat on white sand in the water, seeing his grandfather breaststroke away. Thunder was distant, a fading sound like rusty cannon balls dropping onto a wooden floor and rolling overhead. The boy remained where he was, feeling a hot thrill of nervous excitement flush through him. What was his grandfather doing? Surely he wasn't supposed to swim out there; he couldn't; there was too much drama in the sea and sky, too many shifting colours and waves whipping into the air, some of them

36

momentarily suggesting the dark-grey fin of a shark. So he stayed on shore, saw his grandfather clamber up the beach of the little island, and wave. Nicolas waved back at the naked man against the green-almost-black vegetation and the dark light of the world.

The storm, with its dark watercolours, shaded the blue sea with sadness: Nicolas was leaving tomorrow, returning to his parents. That summer of Caribbean blue was over, and he would never see his grandfather again.

On the roof, Nicolas looked south, to where he had gone so many years ago, knowing even then that his grandmother would outlive his grandfather. He stretched, yawned. The night was cool and quiet. In the distance, to the west, a light signalling on the sea caught his eye. It flashed the same colour as the lightning in his memory, a series of one, two, pause, one, two, then no signal for a few minutes: smugglers.

The island had changed much since his grandfather died. When Nicolas was a boy, a flashing light on the dark sea would have meant alcohol, men avoiding the exorbitant government duty. Now it was cocaine and guns, most of it coming up from Trinidad and Grenada on boats, the cocaine to be taken to the U.S. Air Force Base on the island's north coast, and flown to Puerto Rico, Miami and Atlanta. The last time Nicolas was on the island, the opposition leader, a man long called a communist, had accused the government of complicity. A few weeks later, three U. S. Air Force personnel had been escorted off the island by the D.E.A., and the government, with controlling shares in all radio stations on the island, including one of the only two newspapers, was shown to be responsible for the action leading to the arrests. One month later, on a beach not frequented by tourists, the nude body of a real estate agent had been discovered hacked into nine pieces.

The light continued to flash, slow in the dense night.

Nicolas began to replay bits of the day's conversations in his mind, occasionally adding to the lines he remembered.

Is my father money! Ten thousand dollars!
White lady. Grandmother. Stop! Buy some goats, nuh!
A dollar, Missuss! A dollar!

Watch my father uncle, No-Teeth Joseph, sitting on the box by the church. Is he money too!

But West Indies people could drink, eh Mrs. Roberts?

Everything in moderation, I always say.

Yes, Missuss. I understand.

I am going to have to do something about George.

Indeed.

How's Cuthbert, Albertine?

Oh, still with the rum a little, Mrs. Roberts, but I watches him. That sun and rum don't mix.

Only mad dogs and Englishmen drink in the midday sun.

It is a known fact that the English have the strongest livers in the world – and the Irish.

Nicolas does have a little?

Not me, Albertine, I stick to beers now. But when Grandmother sleeping I swig the sherry in the cabinet between the living room and kitchen.

Don't waste any water. Remember this is a dry island.

If it's brown, flush it down – if it's yellow, let it mellow!

We can explore the reef together, if you like.

What else is there for a small island like this to do?

Getting up from the chair, he grabbed the beer bottle, walked to the roof's edge and flung it into the deep night. A few seconds later, there was a soft crash of glass. The stars were everywhere, some of them slightly inky blue, fat and pulsing and perched low in the night; but above his head their clusters were thick, like the backbone of the universe stretching around the world. He wanted some sherry.

The living room was in darkness; just the flickering of a clinical white light from the kitchen guided him through it.

"Your grandfather used to do that too."

He started, heart seized by adrenaline as he spun around. His grandmother's voice, in the almost melancholy tone it had had on the way to Beggar's Bay, had come from somewhere by the doorway to her bedroom. His grandfather's Berbice chair was set there. He stepped toward it, saw her legs up on one of its long arms and the long black cloak she had wrapped around her for the cool night.

"You scared the… I was thinking."

She lifted something to her face. "Would you like some sherry?"

"Sure."

"You mustn't say that word. Nothing much is these days."

"Did Grandfather really do that, too?"

"That, and other things."

Her voice was relaxed, at ease with him and herself. The melancholy tone had lifted somewhat.

As if sensing his discomfort, she said, "Don't just stand there. Get a glass."

He went to the kitchen, half-expecting some request or admonition to follow him; when he opened the cupboard containing the wine and liqueur glasses, her voice drifted across. "Use the glass you chipped the last time. No point putting more crystal at risk."

He laughed and said, "You know everything."

"Well… I knew I wouldn't catch you out on the level of sherry in the bottle; I can never seem to remember how much I leave in it, but sooner or later a man will leave his mark."

Nicolas touched the tiny bumps of moles on his collarbone.

His grandmother switched on the lamp by her side; it gave a dim glow. He held out his glass and she filled it. "Right. Sit."

He sat in one of the cushioned chairs opposite her. She switched off the lamp. In the dark he could just make out her pale face above the long blackness of the cloak. The wind strengthened and he heard the trees rustling outside. He imagined the land being soothed after the heat it had endured during the day; if the temperature fell enough, there would be rain later, perhaps tomorrow, at least something to prevent the last of the island's green from turning brown like the hides of old horses. He wet his lips with the sherry and said, "I met someone called Rickette, at the beach. You know her?"

"Should I?"

Nicolas was alert. "I just met her today. We had an interesting encounter, you could say."

"Did you notice anything about her?"

"Like what?"

"Oh, anything at all."

"Her moles. But lots of people have them."

She was silent for a while. "I believe your grandfather is the only one who knows the whole story."

He felt tricked by her sherry mood, so he asked, "You're not going to tell me, are you?"

"I told you, only he knows." Starlight glinted off the stem of her sherry glass as she lifted it.

Irritated, but careful of his tone, he said, "You should have been a writer. There's so much you know about here, about Grandfather, the people." He said it as sincerely as he could, wondering if she would detect the lie. Then he added, "You never really liked Grandfather, did you?"

She ignored the question. "He used to write. Poems. Before he met me, while he was courting me, and during our first year of marriage. Then he stopped. It was quite sudden. Some time after your father was born. I guess that's where you got the writing desire from."

"Tell me about Benny."

She sighed, refilled her glass. As if in answer, faint in the night on the sea, they heard a gunshot. Nicolas went over to the wrought-iron gate and looked out into the night.

"Business is picking up," his grandmother said.

"It's eerie. Doesn't it bother you?"

"Not in the least. They stay there; I stay here. But if they see you wandering around at night along the cove below our land, they'll certainly feel as if they have to protect their goods. Anyway, it keeps the area safe." She sipped her sherry.

"Grandfather's poems," Nicolas said. He returned to his chair, hopeful.

"I caught him once, scribbling away one night. He refused to show them to me; acted surprised when I said I wished to see them. I'm sure he was writing them for someone."

"I thought he'd never stopped; just assumed he'd kept on." He was going to say something more, about the last afternoon he'd spent with his grandfather on the point near the cove, the afternoon of the storm, when he'd swum back from the island, but decided against it. He would play her game.

His grandmother said, "The sweetness of the very young… to think that. But age dries up things in you, even poetry, like this damned island. Damned because everything that has ever happened here over the last five hundred years was never meant to happen, was a mistake, wrong. And then suddenly here you are, in it, with no choice but to play the cards you've been dealt… Which meant holding on to everything I could, especially after your grandfather died."

"You aren't going to tell me about Rickette, Benny, the old man you deliberately ignored on the box at the church, why Albertine is so nervous when you give her a lift, the contempt in her voice when she mentioned lawyers today – none of that, are you?"

"I'd prefer not to."

"Never?"

"I'm an old woman now, and I don't want to drag up the past. It's too tiresome. I want to tend my garden and die in peace."

"So who's to tell me?"

But she didn't answer; only looked at him.

He swigged the rest of the sherry in one gulp, enjoying its burning warmth. Outside he heard the sea wind whispering around the solid wooden posts that supported the roof over the porch. He wanted to return to the roof, take the sherry with him, and fall asleep with his thick blanket in the recliner.

"I found them eventually."

"Found?"

"The poems. After that he hid them where I was never able to find them again."

Nicolas waited.

"About his youth in Guyana, the sea here, a woman. They were all beautiful, but sad. It was as if he couldn't forget his swimming days in Guyana, his youth. That's why he swam here so much. He would have lived longer if he'd taken it easy. But we go how we must, I suppose."

"What woman?"

"A woman. I don't know anything more." She stood and picked up the bottle and came over to him. "You can have the rest, if you like. I'm off to the land of Morpheus."

"I think I'm already there." He accepted the sherry. "Thanks."

"Good night."

"'Night."

Big white pillow behind his head, like the whitecaps he saw running on the sea that morning, Nicolas, drowsy, gazed up at the stars. Meteors fell. The night was chilly, and he lay under a thick blanket, sipping sherry. Tina, whining, had tried to climb the ladder with him; he'd taken pity on her, and lugged her up under an arm. Now she lay happily around his feet, keeping them warm, at the end of the recliner. She would not bark: there were no other dogs for miles, and the smugglers' light was gone.

Blacker than the night between the stars, and blacker than he'd ever seen it, was the sea. When his gaze fell from the sky, the sea pulled on him, as the blue had when he was snorkelling just off the reef that afternoon. Something in him wanted to go toward it; but another part of him denied the urge.

A little later, with Tina sleeping at his feet, Nicolas pictured his grandfather swimming back from the island. The rain, after the sea, tasted sweet, as if there was honey in it. And that honey would be dark gold, like rum, the colour of Rickette's skin. His grandfather had arrived at the broken circle of rocks and walked out of the water. When the lightning touched the sea far away, the sand flashed white, ghostly garments beneath their feet. His grandfather went to the large triangular rock he'd looked at earlier and called Nicolas. It was chilly in the rain and the boy shivered. The old man began digging under a section of the rock hollowed like a small cave. After two feet, he'd stopped, tired, looked at Nicolas, smiled, sat back on the sand and gestured at the hole. "Go on, help me." Nicolas began digging, not even thinking to ask what they were digging for, feeling it would soon be revealed and that asking would spoil the joy of discovery. Tiny bits of pink coral began appearing in the damp, shaded sand. Much of the island was coral, a fragile, porous calcified plant rising from great depths of sea and into the air. And they were all supported on its top – Albertine, Grandmother, George, Rickette, everybody. His fingernails had scraped metal – a box with a rectangular wooden handle. He uncovered its width and worked to extract the length. His grandfather went for their clothes, wrung them, and draped them on a bush beneath a nearby tree. He took a key from a pocket of his khaki pants and tossed it on the sand next to Nicolas. The rain became heavy, and nowhere, beyond one hundred and fifty feet, was visible. Nicolas lifted the padlocked metal box, sealed in a thick plastic bag. He untied the neck of the bag, and inserted the key into the padlock, twisting, feeling the rust resist his efforts to unlock it. The key stuck. His grandfather said, "Here, give it here." And he bashed it open with a heavy piece of quartz-coral. They looked at each other, and the naked old man, his remaining hair smooth-soaked on his head, tried to grin, despite the sobriety of his expression. Nicolas was about to open the box when his grandfather took it from him and placed it under the rock. "How is your French coming along at school?"

"Un petit peu, mais mal." Nicolas looked confused. "We're going to read in the rain?"

His grandfather started laughing. He sat back down and laughed until Nicolas began to laugh too. When the boy asked if he were going to have a French lesson in the rain, his grandfather laughed louder.

"But there is too much rain to show you anything. They are some poems and" – he stopped, wiped water from his face – "a picture of someone I want you to meet one day."

Nicolas, disappointed, said nothing. He listened to the rain on the water, watched the sheet of grey-white light the thick rain-drops created as they hit the water by the millions, and imagined it was possible to walk on it to the island his grandfather had swum to. They sat there in the rain, and when they began to feel cold, went back into the water. There was regret in his grandfa-ther's voice when he said, "We should keep this our secret… you'll understand in a few years."

Then, the awkwardness behind them, their shoes on their feet and their clothes bundled under their arms, they ran back to the house in the wet dusk, stumbling up the path. When Nicolas's grandmother met them on the porch, they were breathing heav-ily; she asked them why they had been running around the place like black village boys. She was not amused.

Later, Nicolas, sent to bed early because his grandmother feared he'd get a cold, heard them arguing late into the night.

On a blank page, he started writing in the voice of another.

On a wooden box by the church entrance you could find No-Teeth Joseph. Everyday the man sitting there, as if he waiting to see God face or some such miracle. And so he miserable! When he begging is like he feel you have his money and you must give it back. A white man had leave him money in his will, but No-Teeth never see any of it, because the white man wife hire a dirty lawyer to change the will. Stay a while, don't mind No-Teeth smell bad, he have a story about the white man who make a child with his young sister, the only sister No-Teeth ever had. Now, if you speak to some people they will tell you the white man fuck she; and if you speak to other people, they will tell you they had love for each other. But you mustn't mind them, is only idle gossip them like. Now as sure as my backside big, this true: the child No-Teeth sister had grow up vex with the world; though the mother tell the child who she father was, she didn't tell the child the story at the right time, and didn't tell the right story. And No-Teeth, because he have no teeth, cannot speak too well. So I, Albertine Vivian Edwards, daughter of Glen-Roy Theophilus Edwards, the man who catch and then carry the two-hundred and fifty pound grouper from Beggar's Bay to Wilikies on his back when drought in seventy-three nearly kill that whole village, I will tell you No-Teeth and his sister story. A story about a village, too, about a poor people who lives by the sea.

★

Tina stirred, growled, and Nicolas sat up. He put down the sherry bottle, careful not to make a sound. Tina was staring into the night. She growled again. Nicolas saw nothing, heard nothing. There was nothing but black space, black time and millions of stars curving around the world. He moved forward, closer to Tina; she wagged her tail once, looked at him expectantly. Then she began to whine, without stopping, at the night.

THE VISITORS

High above the sea Trevor sat within the cool walls of his father's house in the mountains outside the city. Across the gulf, Venezuela's high jungle was partly obscured by faint, purple clouds. The dry season had come. The days were hazed, grey-blue water colours drifting across the sky. The squared glints of light on the city buildings below him were like sections of scalpel blades: white light, white heat: the sense of everything there being stripped away, exposed. He ventured out only at night, despite the warnings.

"Who it is who calling?" The maid sounded weary on the telephone.

He hesitated. "Trevor, an old friend. Odette paying you to screen calls now?"

"Just a minute, I think she sleeping."

"Wake her, please," Trevor said. He heard the maid calling Odette, then her voice faded, and he was left with a sound like sea in the distance.

"Hello?" Odette's voice was calm, as if she had been sleeping.

"So, what you doing?"

"Studying, then I dozed off."

"Get much done?"

"Enough. I'll pass."

"You'll pass, and maybe I'll get a job." He laughed.

"Wishful thinking on the second." Her voice was curt. "You should work for your dad. There's nothing else. Not here."

Trevor coughed. Then, tentatively: "Coming over?"

"Yes, once they don't declare a curfew. Some time after lunch?"

"Good," he said. "Good." He felt the day lift inside him a little.

Trevor still lived with his parents; even at his age, twenty-seven, it was considered sensible on the island. There was no need, unless parents and children were bitter toward one another, to move out; no need in Trevor's case to leave the large house, two-storeyed and bone-white, with curving concrete walls that gave it a voluptuous look, unless he was going to get married.

Upstairs in his room of cream walls, of shelves laden with books, there was an unmade bed, a cream-beige carpet and an antique desk, with a little set of drawers mounted on one side. He looked out the window, across the garden, to the quiet public road. It was narrow but not too badly pot-holed. Beyond was a plain lined in the distance by burning mountains, grey in smoke and haze. The razed lower halves of the mountains were ridden with hovels; above them smoke and dust rose at a slight angle. The winds of the dry season, so sensual in the early months when they rustled dry leaves and swayed the elegant green bamboo and wildly bright bougainvillea blossoms, had eased now the season was approaching its end. A great heat, like light with weight, was upon the land. The sky, pale blue with a uniform tint of grey, hadn't changed for weeks.

Every day he would wake at or around noon, damp from the heat, his hair dishevelled and dark eyes tired. The skin beneath them was a little loose and tender, with minute bumps like permanent goose pimples. His mother had warned him he was aging prematurely, that too many late nights could burn out even the most vibrant youth. Trevor would smile. She, he was certain, would get the puffiness and wrinkles around her eyes attended to in Miami this time. His father had shipping business there once or twice a year, and Trevor's mother accompanied him to shop and indulge herself in things unavailable on the island: spas, elegant restaurants and an excellent plastic surgeon. Last year she'd had the sagging, furrowed skin around her neck tucked.

In the garden the light was bright, and seemed to hold the croton and bougainvillea like a lit painting. He stared at the flowers – regularly watered by his mother both early morning and late afternoon, though there was a water shortage every dry season – and the wide, neat lawn ending cleanly on the sides of the driveway, with very few crispy-brown patches.

★

High overhead a helicopter passed. Trevor tried to look at it but the sun hurt his eyes. He'd put out the tape-recorder and a small cooler of beer for Odette, under the sunshade. He wore shorts, a thin grey cotton jersey, and black leather slippers. He wanted to sit in the sun for a while, start his blood gently pulsing after having been sedate behind the concrete walls all morning. He was pale from having been to too many parties and nightclubs.

The helicopter passed again. This time he saw it – lower now, over the plain and heading toward the mountains. Soon it blended into the hard, grey-white light.

"Trevor!"

From the kitchen window, his parent's maid, Bipti, stuck her head out, then an arm, and waved at him to come over. He rose from his chair and sauntered the fifty or so yards. She wore a red and white dress, an orange shirt, large and clumsy fake gold earrings that brushed her collarbones, and bright red lipstick.

"We can't fuck today, you know. Raj coming just now."

He shook his head and laughed. "You. You never stop." He put his hand through the window and caressed her neck. She smiled and bit his hand gently, then lowered it to cup her breast.

Bipti's pitch-black hair was smoothed tightly back into a ponytail, and her features – high cheekbones and full-lipped mouth curving downwards at the sides even when she smiled – were set in curiosity.

"I thought you spend the night by Gibby," she said. "You went out last night?"

"But I didn't stay by Gibby. Gibby is a rum jumbie; if I go on spending too much time with him, God knows what will happen to me." Trevor laughed. "That man is something else."

She removed his hand from her breast and said, "Why you didn't come and see me? Is here I was."

"I thought you might have company."

"You hear that helicopter flying over earlier?"

He nodded. "Must be the army or coast guard."

"Is them damn rebels in the hills they looking for," said Bipti. "I hope they shoot-up their ass."

47

"Best to have you up there searching for them. They won't stand a chance."

"I go eat them alive," she laughed. "What you doing today?"

"Odette said she's coming over."

Bipti cooed and made big eyes at him. "Eh-eh, like your girl coming back! At last she realize you is real man."

"I don't know." Trevor shrugged. "It's good we keep apart most of the time."

"You all will work out, man. Just take things easy."

A motorbike came up the public road, gearing down from high speed in a whining purr.

"That is Raj," Bipti said and left the kitchen.

Raj stopped at the shut gate, saw Trevor and waved. Trevor went to meet him.

"Hey Trevor." Raj, his helmet tucked under one arm, extended the other and, slapping Trevor's palm, gripped his hand in a firm handshake. Raj was slim and had bright, wobbly-looking teeth and soft, dark-wet eyes. He removed a packet of cigarettes and a fluorescent blue plastic lighter from his chequered shirt pocket and, in an affected style reminiscent of old western and kung fu movies, lit a cigarette.

"So how you keeping, Trevor?"

"Can't complain too much."

Raj stroked his black hair and looked up at the house. "You working yet?"

Trevor feigned a sigh. "Not yet."

"Why you don't work for your father? I can't imagine a man not wanting a job like that, yes." Raj scraped the sole of his shoe on the driveway. "Man, you too happy."

"I don't know 'bout that. But a lot of guys my age work for their father."

"So?"

"Maybe I want something different. Still time left to decide."

"Different? Man, look. If I had a chance for a job like that, I would leave 'different' for the weekend."

"It's not enough."

"Well, you could always go up in the cold and study again. Things go improve in a few years here."

Trevor shrugged. "Things bad all over. But the world will go on. Something will happen; I'll do something. Not so old yet, you know."

A door to the house shut and Bipti appeared. "You bring a helmet for me?" she asked, her leather slippers slapping on the driveway.

"It on the bike," Raj said. "Eh-eh, but how you looking so nice?"

"And is you I going out with?" She sucked her teeth. "But when you late, I does show off for Trevor." She winked at Trevor.

"Like I have to watch mehself, Trevor," Raj said, grinning.

"You best believe that. I hear how you was in Graduate Friday night." Bipti turned away from Raj, acting concerned, and addressed Trevor. "Is only a set of old, nasty bat-face woman in the place. And is only reggae they playing – no kaiso. So people does be grinding up slow-slow on each other." She cocked her head to one side and indicated Raj with a self-righteous nod of her chin: "He should be shame to go there."

Trevor said, "Raj man, like you best watch yourself. You know how it have people who like to keep eyes on a sharp man like you."

"Is only cards I playing there." Now he winked at Trevor.

"Cards!" said Bipti. "You wait. I go fix you good." She cuffed him playfully on his arm. Raj winced and sprang back into a kung-fu stance, cigarette between his lips. "Come woman," he said, "make yuh move." When Bipti sprang at him, laughing, he sprang away again, enticing her to pursue him. They pranced across the driveway until Bipti stopped to pick up one of her earrings. "Enough," she said. "All you man too stupid. 'Once a man, twice a child,' as Bob Marley say."

"Like she turning into poet," Raj said, laughing.

"Come, let we go," Bipti said, clipping the earring into place.

Trevor walked with them to the gate. "How's she running?"

"Just like a sweet old bat," Raj said, making eyes at Bipti. As he started the engine, Bipti cuffed him again and got on the bike.

"Where're you going?"

"Cinema!" they said in unison, and sped off. The sound of the engine receded.

Trevor went up to his room. He watched the stretch of public road for a while, wondering when Odette's car would show. Then he lay on his bed and looked out the window. The haze continued to grey the air, erasing the last pale blue of sky. It increased his mood of melancholy, brought on by drinking too much last night and the late hour he'd risen. The quiet, the cool and dull light in his room made him consider sleeping again, though that had not been his conscious reason for coming up the stairs. The walk between his room and the kitchen or the living room was invariably done with his mind elsewhere. On the way to prepare himself breakfast – he never had lunch, preferred a late breakfast and then dinner at seven p.m. – or to catch the world news of weather disasters, failing economies, war, famine, revolution, environmental destruction, the resurgence of diseases thought to be extinct (cholera the latest and spreading northeast from Latin America to his island), he'd be trying to piece together the night before, trying to recall anything worth remembering.

Trevor got out of bed, thirsty, and languidly went downstairs. The silence made him uneasy. It was like a dead weight of air.

He passed the kitchen on his right, went through the door Bipti had used, and out into the sunlight. Heat engulfed him; took him away from the quiet mood that had come to him inside the house.

He wandered over to the sunshade, blades of grass licking the sides of his feet, took a cold beer from the cooler, and nicked off the cap. The aroma of the beer, as a healthy head frothed to the lip of the bottle, was delightfully yeasty. He savoured it before drinking.

The sound of the helicopter drew him out of his doze. A Huey, with mounted M-60 gunships cast downwards on either side, it hovered unsteadily about one hundred feet above the house. At first he thought they were having engine trouble, but then he distinguished two men in the cockpit, one of them using what seemed to be a pair of binoculars. Trevor, thinking they expected a response, waved. Seconds later, the helicopter tilted and rose sharply away; soon it was over the plain, heading toward the mountains, disappearing into the haze.

This dry season a news station had reported pilots were having difficulty with visibility. A group of environmentalists, interviewed in the same broadcast, their warnings interspersed with footage of fires and dust sweeping across the landscape, reminded the government and public that they lived on an island, a tiny island by world standards. One of the environmentalists, his face a blend of anger and wonder, had restated this as if he were revealing information long withheld from the public and which he'd discovered after years of research. Trevor had sympathized with the man. Yet the idea of the dust being blown across the whole island, and hiding it from world-view, appealed to him; the image filled him with a longing he could not define.

He decided to play a tape, have on some music for Odette's arrival; as he was about to do so, he heard the unmistakable sound of her car. He sat up, watched her open the gate, walk gracefully up the driveway, then across the lawn, her long slim legs scissoring beneath her short skirt.

Trevor tensed: he was always stirred anew by her beauty each time they met. He stood and greeted her, kissing a mole close to her mouth.

"So, how are you?" Her tone was smug, and a bit formal.

He recognized her mood; he would have to be quite charming today. He shrugged and smiled modestly, the way he had when they'd first met.

"I hope you don't have any expectations," she said. "I am bleeding like an abattoir."

His eyes went wide in mock astonishment. "Really? How terrible. Does it hurt?"

Odette, fingers intertwined and resting on her lap, had a faint smile at the corners of her mouth. He opened two beers and put one on the table in front of her.

She leaned back into her chair and considered him. "So, you getting a job soon or what?"

Trevor looked away above her head. The casual way she'd asked, expecting no more information than she already had, made him wonder about surprising her – telling her of some imminent interview. Could he redeem himself? The idea titillated him. If he could tell it with sufficient seriousness, she might respect him more, and see him more often.

"Still looking," he said. "I've got to find the right thing. I hate flitting about from job to job."

"Yes. Commitment. That's what we want in our lives." She wasn't smiling now.

"Exactly. What our poor, damaged island needs."

Odette leaned forward. "Have you thought about going back to university, starting graduate study?"

"All too often." The humour left his eyes. Then he said: "But Dad would have to pay… You know, some people are too willing to see another's way of living as irresponsible. It gives them a sense of importance. He was so insulted when I turned down his offer to work with him."

"Why did you?"

He fidgeted. "I had my reasons. Sometimes things are not what they seem." Trevor looked at the house.

Her voice rose. "Whatever. The fact remains that you lack a career."

"This is a great crime. What shall we do? But I am responsible: I stay out of trouble." He opened two more beers, handed her one, and began to peel the label of his.

"That's easy." She waved toward the house.

"You can't be sure. If you saw me more, then maybe you would know the truth."

"You don't give me good reasons to see you more, Trevor."

"It bothers you a lot that I didn't accept my dad's offer, right?"

She ignored him.

A hot breeze came from the plain. Trevor felt dust particles collecting on his face and arms. He sipped his beer and tilted himself back in his chair. Odette put her head back and looked at him through half-closed eyes. He saw the hovels as dabs of pastels on the mountains. High above vultures circled in a thermal, their rise and fall nearly imperceptible through the haze. He was on the verge of suggesting she stay for the weekend when a thunderous thwacking alarmed them. Rising above the plain, detaching from immense swirls of dust, the helicopter passed over the house and dipped beyond it, the mutilating sound of its blades fading instantly.

"We are a nation of fun and games," said Odette.

"It could be serious; they've been flying around here all morning. But not like that."

The thwacking resumed. The helicopter was not visible, but the sound was deafening. Then at the far end of the house's roof, above his parent's bedroom, it showed, moving very slowly, whipping the plants flat and bending and ruffling the trees.

"Your mother's roses!" Odette shouted.

"What?"

She repeated herself.

"Oh fuck," and he ran, waving his arms. When he was sure they could see him clearly, he started pointing at the open lawn, bending his arm at the elbow again and again. "Go there!" he yelled, suddenly realizing that only the mouthing of the words mattered. One of the men leaned out of the helicopter and put a hand to his ear. By looking more attentively at Trevor, he eventually got the message and nudged the pilot. The helicopter, like a colossal dragonfly, shifted over to the lawn where, in a gradual increase in whining and a gradual decrease in thwacking, it descended onto the lawn with a bump. The power was shut off but the machine continued to whine for a while.

The men took their time in getting out. Trevor could see them fumbling with an M-16 rifle. The man who'd understood Trevor's directions stepped onto the lawn and said to the other, "Is all right, leave it. Just rest it down and come out."

A short bald man, corpulent and dressed in fatigues, the trousers too long for him, hopped onto the lawn and jogged, in knockkneed fashion, to keep up with his taller, slim associate. The associate was dressed in the uniform of a high-ranking army officer and smiled a wide, easy smile at Trevor and Odette. With a swagger, he said, "Sorry to drop in like this." Both men had holstered pistols on their waists.

Trevor introduced himself and Odette. She made a low, derisive sound in her throat.

"And I'm Captain Guzman," said the high-ranking officer. "And this," he indicated the clownish figure huffing and puffing towards them, "is Officer Besson."

Besson halted and smiled, at the same time removing a bright yellow handkerchief from a back pocket. There was a space between his front teeth; it reinforced his clownishness. He extended his hand to Odette, shook hers up and down, a single, unbroken movement. He mopped his shaved head with the handkerchief, nodded, still smiling at Trevor, then seeing the beers on the table, said, "Guz, man, I could real use a cold drink."

Trevor invited them to sit, and, offering beer all round, asked what kind of patrol they were on.

Officer Besson guzzled his beer, head thrown back, the whites of his eyes bulging at first, then slowly half-closing in contentment.

"Ah," he said, and belched. "This is what I call a breeze. But inside the belly." He patted his protruding stomach, fingers caressing it in circular motion.

Guzman said, "We just keeping an eye out for any suspicious activities. You know how things are these days. We get a report of guerrillas in the hills last night. You see anybody who looking as if they looking for trouble recently?"

Trevor thought: Yes. You, me, and pretty much the whole damned, fucking island.

Guzman sipped his beer. He had an ascetic appearance. His local diction was tinged with an American accent; and he had an odd shoulder shrug, a jerky movement of annoyance.

"You could work your way from parliament down, across and back up – through every level of society – and find people looking for trouble," Odette said.

"Exactly so," Besson said. "That is why we have to be on *strickess* alert at all times." His puffy face creased; mimicking surprise, he held up his beer bottle, the bottom angled just above his eyes: "But eh-eh, Guz, like my beer finish."

Somewhat amused, Trevor got another beer for Besson. He expected no thanks and got none. "You guys need a break," he said.

"Boy," Guzman said, "is true."

Besson exhaled lengthily, and said, "*If.*"

Odette nudged Trevor under the table with her foot, but before he could look at her, Besson interrupted.

"You know, is a funny thing. But every time we fly over the

northern part of the island, we does chop a vulture, without fail." And he slashed the air in front of him.

"Another thing!" Besson continued, pointing his index finger upwards, "I believe the reason for chopping a vulture or two every time we fly over is that it have more vulture here than in other areas of the island."

"Very true," Guzman said, nodding.

"Imagine that," Besson said, taking out his yellow handkerchief and mopping his head. "Imagine that."

Trevor wanted to laugh. What else was there to do? Odette observed Besson blankly. Besson frowned at her.

"He put that vulture business here to you all today," Guzman said, placing his empty bottle on the table. "Today." He tapped his hand on the table to leave no doubt that it was indeed today Besson had put it.

"Well –" Trevor began. Odette glared at him.

"Why it have more vulture in the northern part of the island than in the central and southern part?" Besson said, staring at the top of the sunshade. "I will tell you why. Is because the northern range have more affluence than the other ranges! More rich people lives here than anywhere else – therefore," he huffed, eyes resting on Odette, "there is more waste product available for the vulture!"

He sat back, pleased with himself. The whites of his eyes rolled upwards, his mouth fell open – head tilting back – and a long, low wheeze of laughter left him.

"Exactly," Guzman said. "You're one hundred percent correct."

"Any fool could tell you that," Besson said, giving a palm-up, horizontal flick of his wrist.

"So I see," Odette said.

Trevor winced. Besson and Guzman seemed oblivious.

"You guys hit any lately?" Trevor asked quickly.

"Two," Guzman said. "This morning. Look. You could even see blood on the helicopter."

"They go dupf!" said Besson, hitting the table, "and instant blood on the windshield. We does have to hose it down every day. Not so, Guz?"

Guzman nodded. "How they so damned stupid to see a big

helicopter flying to them and not get out the way, eh? Answer me that one, Besson."

Besson's eyebrows rose and he grinned at Guzman.

Odette stood, placed her empty bottle on the table, got another beer, and said to Trevor firmly, "I'll be inside."

She walked up the incline to the kitchen door, not once looking back, went into the house and slammed the door.

Besson and Guzman were silent. Trevor could feel a new tension building. But he offered them more beer. It was something to do; it was something to delay, maybe, the brutal power they possessed. Opening the cooler again to get the beer, he realised the time left was in a beer – Besson's beer since he drank so quickly. Though Guzman was in control, Besson would set the pace, give the signal; he was the impatient one, the initiator.

"I hear you say 'guys'. You study in America?" Guzman asked. "I study in the Carolinas." He smiled. "Where you study?"

"Boston," Trevor said.

"So you must work with your old man," Guzman said.

Besson, fidgeting now, his beer almost finished, clasped his hands on his stomach, looked straight at Trevor and said, "But of course. Of course. He have it made, man. You think if my father had a big house so I would be flying round this island looking for guerrillas to shoot?" He sucked his teeth – a bubbly, hissing sound. "Man, you making joke."

"You?" laughed Guzman. "You would find some slackness to hook up in."

Trevor said, "No, I don't work with my father."

"You looking at two big men like we, men of the Defence Force in a state of emergency, and lying so bold face?"

Trevor felt the honesty of his reply bring on an unfamiliar force in him: defiance. It pleased him to see Besson annoyed by his answer. Yet he knew it was tactless.

"A big, nice house," Guzman said; "money, security and so on. You must be working for your father. You must want a piece of this action, man. You set for this life and the next."

"I'm not the business kind," said Trevor.

"Not the business kind," Besson said. "What kind of business it is exactly?"

"Shipping."

"How you could be so stupid to miss out on that?" Guzman pointed at the house. "Or part of it. Your father have too much to pass on."

Trevor gave no response.

"He will get it anyway," Besson said. And then: "Shipping..." Besson was thoughtful.

"But maybe not the business," Guzman said. "It must be a good business, judging by the house. How you could not want it?"

There was nothing else to say or do, and he did not want to continue waiting. With an irritated expression, Trevor rose, impatient for them to end their stay or begin their final act. Besson leaned forward, his fat face tensing in anger, and also rose; right hand curling around the gun on his hip. With an absurd kind of relief, Trevor watched him when he said: "We have reason to believe you are bringing arms into the country. Drugs also. We go search the house for evidence now."

He never took the gun out; simply kept his hand on the butt. Guzman stepped away from them and stood quietly. Besson came over and nudged Trevor with his other hand. "Move," he said. Trevor, though feeling he should protest, ask questions, was silent.

Guzman remained several paces behind Besson. They entered the cooler air of the house, and Trevor became uncannily aware of the familiar scents. He led them into the living room, not really knowing why – perhaps because it was a larger area they would be more comfortable – and all the absurdity, every comic nuance of their arrival, left him. He was afraid: his retreat, his sanctuary, the place he had made himself in – this large, cool, pale house set up and away from the city – had been penetrated. When Besson kicked him hard in the foot, the tip of the boot bruising bone above ankle, he was almost grateful, as he dropped to the floor, for the distraction of physical agony.

Guzman, hands on hips, looked about him. "Nice," he said. "Real nice. You have anything to eat in the fridge, boy?"

Trevor, his voice squeezed by pain, said, "Over there," and pointed to the kitchen. Guzman went in and began fumbling in the refrigerator.

"Where the girl?" asked Besson.

Trevor said nothing.

The look on Besson's face as he yanked him up from the floor, made Trevor wonder how one man could hate another so much without knowing him. He thought he would be killed then. He cowered when Besson held the gun at his throat. It was too much: before Besson could repeat the demand, Trevor said, "Take anything you want. Wreck the whole damn place. Burn the house. I have nothing to do with my father."

"Where the girl?" Besson repeated.

Guzman strolled back in, munching on a sandwich. He began to search through a bureau in the small passageway that led to the study. Sheaves of old bills and other documents Trevor had no idea about billowed upwards into the still air, flung from his right hand. Trevor knew he would make his way to the study soon, and there, if he could open the safe, he might find what he was looking for.

Guzman, placing the last morsel of the sandwich between his neat lips, said: "There's nothing, Besson. Looking useless." But the words were spoken casually. Then, seriously, he said: "Have a sandwich instead of the girl, Besson. You know we can't go too far."

When Besson stepped back and pointed the gun at him, Trevor said, "She must have left." He stared straight at Besson now, relieved to be alive, and confident he would stay that way in Guzman's presence. He stared at Besson's bulging eyes, the sweat on his upper lip, and the way he worked his tongue beneath the lips.

Besson holstered his gun, stepped toward Trevor, and kicked him in the shin again. Trevor fell to the ground, cursed, and grabbed the injury, rubbing furiously and asking, "What do you want? What do you want? There's a safe in there, why don't you blast it open?"

Reluctantly, Besson turned away. Trevor decided that when they left, as Guzman seemed to want, he would call the police. The impulse to report the brutality, the crime: it was something he could do. He began to watch Guzman and Besson carefully: their weapons, clothes and faces. They paid him no attention.

The bruise pained enough to make him limp as they took him outside. Besson – indifferent to Trevor's presence, to what he might think and repeat about what he was saying – spoke to Guzman about links yet to be made for security, how the politicians had had every chance and the absolute need for drastic changes in infrastructure.

Trevor wasn't really listening to Besson, though he thought he should. He concentrated on preparing himself to memorize the registration number on the helicopter.

At the door of the cockpit, Besson stopped and spoke directly to Trevor. "This a small island, boy, and the future not looking too hot. Party and Carnival don't solve everything. And the cholera coming soon." Then: "Watch the registration, boy. Watch it good."

Trevor did.

The rotor began turning, the whine of the machine increasing as the blades mutilated the air with huge slices. The familiar thwack sounded. The tumult of air forced Trevor backwards; and as the aircraft rose a slow motion jump of a few feet, Besson pointed gun-shaped fingers and hand at Trevor, and jerked his index finger up and down, his lips pursing silent shots. Trevor stood there until they slipped back up into the sky and were swallowed by the grey dust.

Inside he wrote down the registration number and left the accumulation of bills and receipts on the floor. In the study he found the telephone connection untouched. He called police headquarters and spoke to a man who seemed to doubt the story of the helicopter landing on the lawn.

"Yes," he said, when Trevor tried to communicate the seriousness of the matter. "I'll pass it on to the Commissioner."

"Please do," Trevor said. "I think it would – no. Wait. Let me speak to him." And he gave his father's name, one the Police Commissioner would be sure to know from the social functions of those in business and politics. The officer asked him to repeat his father's name, and then put him through to another officer, who screened him.

A pleasant, wheezy voice came on. Trevor introduced himself unnecessarily, to which the Commissioner responded,

"Ah." He asked some courteous questions: how was his father, his mother.

When Trevor had told him everything, he said, "Yes, yes. We have some subversive groups in the country... you know how it is... a weak leader... no support from the grass roots. Perhaps you can tell your father to contact me from Miami as soon as possible. I'm sure he'd want to get it cleared up right away."

"Of course."

"Good. I'll have two officers up there in about half an hour."

"I've left everything alone."

The Commissioner hung up.

Trevor went into the study. Guzman had rummaged out the desk and opened the cupboard doors at the bottom of the bookshelves. The safe was visible, locked; no attempt had been made to open it.

The police officers never came.

Trevor opened the door to his room. He paused to look at Odette on his bed, her back to him. He shut the door and she turned, her eyes registering him through half-conscious slits. The afternoon had worn on; the room was dim; and the white walls in the late light were the colour of ancient bones.

He went to the window. The mood, the moment for him and her, was gone. He would make no effort to revive it. Soon, with night and her absence, other possibilities would arrive. Gibby would call; if not, he would call Gibby. It did not matter: the possibilities were there. But he wondered, thinking of Besson and Guzman, and his father, how much longer it would last.

A puff of cool air entered the window. He stared out through the haze to the city; it was crowded and filthy, with huge parts in decay, as if waiting to be burnt. Some of the money from the last oil boom had been splurged on a skyline of two tall cylindrical buildings, a poor imitation of Caracas and San Juan. The gutters shone with green muck. Small children drowned every rainy season in the huge drains built to flush the slums above the city. Beggars and wild men roamed the capital and suburbs, muttering threats to passers-by.

He continued to look out the window at the dust, drifting now in a gentle breeze, until he heard a murmur, a sudden swish of the sheets, a sharp intake of breath: Odette was dreaming. In sleep – her face twitching, fingers moving – her fear took over. His came at noon when he woke, when he was preparing himself for another day.

"Have they gone?" Odette asked.

Her voice was soft, strangely distanced in his memory, as if the process of their disintegration had long since passed. It startled him. He sank into the cushioned chair at the window. With her dark hair and eyes he'd once found so dear, she now added to the melancholy mood with the sound of her voice, the turn of her head and the slow, relaxed stretching of her limbs. He knew then that she was already retreating, becoming an experience of the past. He had an odd desire to thank her and ask her to leave, for now he was certain he would never pursue anything she wanted for them from his father. They were, at last, finished.

"They've gone," Trevor said.

"What did they want?"

"Well, things are a bit of a mess." He wanted to smile at the understatement.

She moved to the edge of the bed. "Why'd you let it go on?"

He shrugged. "They were entertaining. And they were armed."

"You mean you enjoyed it?"

"For a while, I suppose."

"What happened after I left? Did they rough you up?"

"Of course."

"And did you enjoy that?"

The light in the garden had dimmed further, and colour was fading, ghosting in the grey. Soon, he sighted evening's first sign: a faint purple over the city, like a sky about to bleed. The evening chill would come and he would be left alone. The thought pleased him.

"I should be going," Odette said.

At the bottom of the stairs, he showed her the results of Besson and Guzman's visit.

"Why didn't you just leave? I did."

"They didn't make me angry; they were entertaining. I told you." But he sighed, then shrugged again. "I don't know."

61

"Did you call the police?"

He nodded. "Said they'd send someone up."

"Why do you suppose they did this?"

He didn't see the point in telling her his guesses. "Bored, I think, or just a little practice for the revolution. Whatever."

"And they didn't take anything?"

"No."

The ease with which they had committed the violation came to him fully now. What did they know about his father?

"Do you want me to follow you home?" he asked.

"I can take care of myself."

Back in his room, looking at the mountains becoming more defined, and the haze changing to faint purple, he thought about nothing. He was waiting for the time when his evening mood would envelop him, promising a night's adventure.

Raj's motorbike appeared on the public road, with Bipti hunched around him. The machine slowed and stopped at the gate, which Bipti opened. They walked up the driveway and across the lawn. At the garden hose, Bipti turned and shouted up at him, then bent to turn on the pipe. Raj looked up and shouted: "Good picture! Good picture!" and waved. Bipti sprayed him with water, and they began to play, wetting each other intermittently as they watered the garden. Afterwards, going to Bipti's room, they looked up at him again and waved. He returned the gesture.

Under a hot shower he brushed his teeth, cut his fingernails. The hot water massaged his neck and shoulders. He soaped languorously, allowing the foam to froth and bubble all over. After rinsing, he thrust his head into a large fluffy towel and rubbed vigorously. He was refreshed, the beers had worn off, and now he wanted something new. He was not hungry.

Downstairs he mixed a vodka-and-tonic, stronger than normal, came back upstairs, dressed, and sat at the window. Twilight was complete. A few stars were out, and the haze, especially down by the city, held the last of the blue-black, purple light. The sun was sinking behind Venezuela and silhouetting a small cluster of islands between. He picked up the drink, cold and swathed in condensation.

Someone had told him – he could not remember who or where, exactly – was it somewhere in the Windward Islands at a party on someone's yacht? – most of the haze at this time of year was dust, which had risen in huge storms in the Sahara, then moved southwest across the Atlantic. This wind was called the Harmattan. Ever since, Trevor had welcomed each dry season with a kind of reverence for the distance the dust had travelled, and the image of swirling grainy wind, like wheat in the sky. But now he imagined the dust collecting through villages and cities, sweeping over vast lands long pregnant with dead; and the new dead, disintegrating finally, into minute particles that became buoyant and wandering.

THE WHITE PEOPLE MAID

Again and again Madam would ask me, *Cynthia, have you seen my cell phone?* And she setting up she face as if I don't have cell phone so must thief white people own. Last week it was the gold bracelet, week before the bag of bird pepper she was to give Mrs. Huggins.

The boldface bitch.

But the real joke is, when Mrs. Gomes (that is she name, but she better known to me as Old Bitch) find what it is she looking for, I does stop whatever I doing, fold up my arms good and proper, and watch Old Bitch hard. And not once she find the decency to apologize to me! Not once at all. But sometimes I notice she shame, eyes low and avoiding mine, a blush on she cheeks and neck. Is a good thing the woman Catholic, yes, so she not above feeling guilt, because if I didn't know better, I would feel real pressure to *buss* she head with the oversize stainless steel pot she does use, and so proud of, when cooking for she white, rich friends.

Now you must think I is a ungrateful black woman who never know she place in the high society area I working in. But let me tell you something. Was over a year I went there every Wednesday morning to sweep, do laundry, wash dishes, dust, make up bed, oftentimes cook, mop, talk to Old Bitch when she lonely – which is plenty times these days; she husband pass twenty years now – help bring in groceries, and walk over to the daughter flat – five doors down in this compound these high society people living in – to borrow this-that-and-the-other. I was always doing something for somebody here, but mostly for Mrs. Gomes and she daughter, who I does call Paris Hilton because of the way that woman does move. I never see trouble in a woman like this daughter, which is how most of the confusion with the cell phone, and everything else, really start.

The daughter didn't always live here in this compound, she come from up by Cascade side. She and she husband, a Mr. Adamson, was building a house and paying rent for the one in Cascade before coming here. The new one they build, they build in Hale Land Park, a pretty area for rich people. When the house finish the daughter decide to rent it and come and live in a two storey here, five doors down from she mother place. And Lord, from the time that daughter reach, my trouble start. Sometime ten times a day I walking from the Madam flat to the daughter own and back. These white people like to see black people work, you hear. I thought that I uses to have trouble with Old Bitch, but like the Devil poison the woman heart when the daughter settle here. Them two fight like cat and dog, and even stop talking for over three months! Was real bad, something about who was to babysit the daughter two children a evening. The daughter say Old Bitch had *say* she had agree to mind the children a Saturday night. Anyway, the new year reach, and you know how these Catholic and them is – they can't stay vex with each other too long, must be they feel the good Lord watching them in truth, so when Carnival season begin they was speaking with one another again and taking turn watching the children.

Yes now, to get back to the story. Was a early afternoon, smoke drifting through the neighbourhood and beyond, as if the Prime Minister issue a order to burn down the whole damn island (that is how the Madam does call it when she vex). Old Bitch was watching she soaps on TV, lying down on the couch in the living-room, she head prop up with two-three pillows. But what I didn't notice too good that day was that Old Bitch face was set up like the Opposition Leader own when he in Parliament and feel he could get the whole country to swallow the biggest set of non-sense since we first Prime Minister Eric Williams bawl, *Massa day done!* I didn't notice Old Bitch face too much at the time, as I say, but it turn out to be real important. When you see a man, or a woman, as was the case here, with a look like they discover gold in their backyard and they don't want nobody to know and they enjoying keeping the secret, is a troubling thing, especially for me who was so use to working for a woman who *always* miserable! At first I was glad when I find she happy-happy. Was like a new day, as if a new time was about to begin, as if the good Lord had smile on this woman *at last*, as if maybe she do something good in this wicked old world we all living in.

That whole morning I count my blessings. I wasn't even calling she Old Bitch to myself; was only Madam this and Madam that. I say to myself, *Like she turn Buddhist or something?* So calm and peaceful the woman was, like a flower, never mind it wrinkle and two-three petal dropping off, was a real nice spirit coming from inside she and putting a glow around everything she say and do. Man look, I even start to hear the birds singing in the garden for the first time, or maybe I uses to hear them from before but did never know I was hearing them because of the bitching Old Bitch uses to bitch.

When two o'clock reach that afternoon, the daughter come quiet-quiet by the kitchen window and ask, *Cynthia, Mummy there?* I was washing dishes and she catch me by surprise, and a glass in my hand slip and break in the sink. Old Bitch hear it, but she didn't mind! She say, *Cynthia, something broke?*

Yes, Madam, I say. *A glass. I sorry, but Mrs. Adamson frighten me. Look she here for you.*

From the time the daughter walk in and sit down, I know something wrong. I catch the little Paris Hilton bitch watching me like she must be feel I working for CIA or Al Qaeda.

After a five minutes or so, the Madam and she daughter get up and step outside onto the little porch just after the living-room. Was then I know they had private business to discuss. They stay there for about half hour, and the Madam never call me to ask for a little tea for she and she daughter, something they always does when they sitting inside the living-room on a afternoon. The Madam doesn't go outside on the porch until it gets cooler, around five or so. That day they went out on the porch, was a quarter past two.

I was still in the kitchen when the daughter leave. As she was leaving, she stop and ask me, *Cynthia, when you were over by me yesterday, did you see an earring like this?* And she remove a pretty-pretty diamond earring from the leather handbag she always carrying around as if she modelling the stupid thing.

She watch me straight in my face when I say no, and ask, *You sure?*

Yes, I say, watching she back in she face.

She turn and start to walk off down the little corridor leading out of Madam flat. I follow behind her and say, *Mrs. Adamson, I does not steal people jewellery.*

Glad to hear it, she say, not even bothering to look back at me, she fake, blonde Paris Hilton hairstyle swinging right to left like a L'Diablesse backside.

And is true: I doesn't steal jewellery.

The daughter marry a funny looking white man who come out from England long time; he resemble a Arab, but he have the name Adamson, and I sure he feel from the time he set eyes on she that she must be Paris Hilton sister or something so, because he run she down like she was the last woman on God earth. He is not a bad man. I like him. He does talk to me sometimes, especially when Paris and Old Bitch giving him hell, which is often times these days. When I see him out by the compound pool, staring dreamy-dreamy up at the mountains with the two big Arab eye he have, looking up the valley to the north and smoking cigar, he does have a tired, droopy look on he face, as if the whole world bringing him down. Yet he does always say hello to me when I passing in the road, ask me how things going with the Madam.

Cynthia, you all right?

Yes, Mr. Adamson, sir.

Madam treating you good?

Things okay. I managing. But you know how it is. The Madam does misplace things plenty, and often times she does lend them to she daughter. And I back and forth between the two flat so much, I can't keep watch on all the people about the place.

One day I ask him, *Mr. Adamson, sir, you feel I thief anything from the Madam or Mrs. Adamson?*

He shake his head. *No*, he say. *Madam getting on now, she is forgetting things. But Mrs. Adamson say she having trouble with you.*

Was then I swear on my soul to him that I never take anything from his home, nothing what belonging to anybody else. Nothing at all. I watch him. And I know he believe me.

The daughter make two child with Mr. Adamson – bam bam! – and you would never think this woman make them two little ones. I never see a woman recover she looks after pregnancy so! She must be sell she soul to the Devil to get back such a nice figure. No lie. You know how some people feel God watching out for them? Well, that is not the case here at all, mark my words. Here, in Trinidad, is the Devil what watching people – first order of the day for plenty damn people, if you ask me. Whosoever feel God minding them must be get buss head. Like they feel God have time to worry about them and they stupidness? He busy elsewhere; it have too many things He doing. If you study your brains, is like you is a tiny, tiny ant in the desert in Africa somewhere, and God in a next part of the universe – far far away – you catch what I saying? But that don't mean He can't reach here, even in this crazy-ass Trinidad. I feel He does come here sometimes. But to *feel* He have business with all them brazen, old white bitch it have about the place, all them white-ass, Port-of-Spain, Catholic housewife? That is blasphemy – *for so!*

But I was telling you about the Madam, the day the good Lord see fit for she not to be a Old Bitch – well, at least for a few hours. So hear what happen.

You know how this island is – from since long time Trinidad always a place for bacchanal, eh. My mother Janice uses to say it all start up when the Yankee and them reach Trinidad in the last big war England and America had with Germany. And just when you think you get use to the madness, to the shit-hounds (that is what Madam does call them), to the noise and the wild, let-go-beast man it have roaming all about, some driving Mercedes and BMW, is like a Lara bat hit you from behind and you gone clear over the pavilion, sailing like a cork ball, and now you falling down, collapsing, eye and them closing up, and your mind switching off. Just so my mother Janice dead. Trinidad *hit* she for six. Always taking on, taking on – worries for so that woman had! Make my father run like crab by the time I turn fifteen and start with boys. The woman uses to talk nonstop about every problem it have in this mad-ass island. My father Derrick would hold his head like it going to explode and bawl, *Oh God, Janice! Leave the girl alone! Forget about Trinidad and all it problems; the good Lord know what he doing!*

Was holy terrors in that house I grow up in. And Lord, the

amount of fight they fight, my parents. You would have think my father had love rum, but wasn't so. He was a religious man, always in Church first thing Sunday morning, don't mind it raining and thundering. He there. He was devote to his routine, a simple man, who realize God testing him when my mother pass three years quarrelling with everything under the sun. But the test wasn't to remain living with she, it was to catch himself and run far, far away, to leave she ass behind. And to *stay* away from she.

Every now and again he does send me a little something to help with Christmas and Carnival, and I does visit him every New Year's, and sometimes weekends every few months.

Living in this Trinidad is a stressful thing. Don't mind if you religious-religious, time bound to come when you will put down a good cuss – but I doesn't cuss like them let-go-beast it have all about, especially them Trini man who feel they could say anything to anybody and pull out the little gun they have and discharge bullet in people car, foot, leg, and backside – just what happen in the pharmacy down the road by the corner one afternoon last week when Old Bitch send me for some sleeping tablets.

Imagine, you walking down the road to the pharmacy not three hundred yards from Old Bitch flat, walking in hot sun, fire burning on the mountains, clouds of dust all about, plenty car speeding up and down like the drivers on crack, the watchman at the guard hut pose up and shaking he backside to the latest Carnival tune on the radio, the two security poles up so anybody could come in the compound and make trouble, and I walking, yes I walking, minding my own business. But like the whole island gone crazy and is every man for himself and God against all, and as I get to the pharmacy door, I stop for the guard inside to see I is woman and woman alone and that I not coming inside to rape, kill, and shoot-up the people place, and then the door open, and *whoosh!* – man, that cool air like it lift me up and carry my heat-up self into another world. Is peace now, and I in heaven, and confident with the hundred dollars in my pocket what Madam give me. I walking about the aisles and stopping there, here, and all about, for I resting you see, catching mehself, looking like I can't make up my mind or remember what to get – vitamins,

Chinee oil, pampers for Paris Hilton children, mosquito spray, shampoo, toothpaste, bath soap, hair spray – and I paying no mind as yet to the sleeping tablets the lady at the drugs counter know I come to get (for mostly that is what the Madam does send me for), and is like the drugs counter lady know what I doing, for she only smiling when I watch she, as if she know my troubles. She must be my guardian angel, for she don't trouble me – and *oui papa*, I does feel myself come back to me, my mind ease off my worries. Is like the part of me that so like my mother step aside – she gone, take she blasted self away like a soucouyant that see day coming and have to fly.

Was a day so, when two young boys push past a lady going out the pharmacy, and before I know what going on, the two of them screaming and shouting at everybody, one with a gun pointing at the guard, the other with a cutlass and he waving it. They making people take out they money and put it in a bag. Young boys, you know, one with his head shave, the other with hair growing back, little pigtails sprouting like worms wriggling up out of the earth. I freeze. So quiet and still I was from fear it was like my spirit had leave the pharmacy, leave me there with them young hooligans. Within a minute, maybe two, they shoot the guard, a Indian, thief everybody money except mine – it was as if they never even see me, as if I have nothing to give – and chop a "elderly woman", the papers say later, who try to pull she purse away from the boy with the bag. I see the woman hand leave her body and drop on the ground. I doubt the boy had education, but he did know how to use that cutlass, yes. The woman fall and stay silent. She and the guard dead. The boys shoot open the door to leave, not bothering in the rush to search the guard for remote or keys for the door.

After the boys leave, after the cashiers and them start to cry and bawl for police, I watch everybody like in a dream and walk out, nobody telling me to stop, out the door I gone, walking in hot sun back to Madam place, without the sleeping tablets. And as far as I know, nobody ever call me to be witness.

On the way back I panic and try to call Madam on she landline from my cell phone. Was only away from the pharmacy I feel as if I coming back down to earth. I catch myself and feel I have to try and do something. So I try to call Madam. And while I pressing the numbers on the cell phone it slip from my hand and fall on the pavement by the railing over the big gutter like a river it have as you heading to Madam compound. The cell phone bounce, little piece chip off, and it drop into the nasty water below what coming down from Hale Land Park side, and it disappear.

Right there by the roadside I stop and look up at the sky and ask the Lord why he so. Like He don't have a heart, is as if black people eh get enough torment yet and the Lord Heself playing Devil with we. I had a good mind to cuss He, the Devil, Jesus, Joseph and Mary, and everybody come down, but I walk up the hill past the entrance to Madam compound, and I keep on going, rising above the Saddle Road where the pharmacy is, above the compound too, and when I catch myself, I seeing the sea in the Gulf of Paria, and so pretty it look you might never think it have so much rubbish and old nasty history in it.

And on the hill overlooking the city, on the hill overlooking the sea, on the hill overlooking Central Trinidad, I cry for this whole blasted island. I cry for my cell phone; I cry for my father who never make his dream come true – to be a teacher in Fatima College; I cry for my mother early death; I cry for Old Bitch how she so lonely and can't get a man again; I cry for the poor children it have in this island – the richest country in the Caribbean – and I cry for the future, and the past. And then I cry for myself, for the education I never get.

When darkness fall, is only then I start to feel a little better, so I go back down the hill part way, make a right, and walk through the rich people area known as Fairways. Nobody could see me, and I only saying, Lord, let me reach by Valleton Ave and Saddle Road, I will catch maxi-taxi there and go home and pray thanks I still have my life.

While I walking along the road through Fairways, passing all the mansion it have about, everything was quiet-quiet, as if everybody already hear about the robbery and keeping safe inside. Then the stars appear, pretty-pretty, but I didn't stop to watch them, I walking, straight and proper to Valleton Ave, hoping all would be well from now and that I would reach home safe and see my father smiling tomorrow at some calypso it have playing on the radio for the Carnival just round the corner.

I had just reach about halfway to Valleton when I see a Midnight Robber coming up the road. Well Lord, what is this? Carnival eh reach yet but so these people playing they Mas. And too besides, I had thought the Robber was no more. In this modern Trinidad, my father say, everything that is the real Trinidad getting throw way.

But the Robber *was* there. He stand tall, a man dress up in one of them big sombrero hat and a long black cloak hanging a few inches above his feet, showing the old sneakers he wearing. I didn't see what the Robber really had hanging all round the edge of his sombrero, for I was too 'fraid to look close. They was decoration, like Christmas bulbs or something so. Is only when he finish talk and move a little more in the street light, after giving he little show, that I notice what it was the man had hanging round his head. As he come abreast of me, he stop like a soldier under the street light and introduce heself.

Ah! Good evenin', Madam. I am the resurrection of Lazarus, and I have strode across the last two millenniums to alight in the souls of Magellan and Raleigh, both of them I am, and both of them I am not, for I am Lazarus, Lord of Death! who has tricked both life and death and found a home here in this dread Trinidad for many a year now. I travel in your dreams to be here! I have argued with God, struck down the Devil, and Jesus was my playmate… before I make him into a curry roti and eat him all up!

In 1492 when Columbus discover the New World, I was there with a guiding hand. The Indians confided in me they did not like Columbus and his men, because they didn't bathe often, and the Indians never soften on that! The Europeans had a bad scent from a strange sea, and that cause so much bloodshed, you see. And when the Europeans and them start to fight, and all the ships and souls get bent, all the fight they fight in their big ships fill up the sea with bodies of black and white men – and all their blood! – so I did clap my hands with glee, and then I rent a tent and had a rest! But this is no jest! What a carnival of corpses became the Caribbean Sea! A rainbow of black and white and red, for all to see! – the lovely and most distinguished colours of our national flag! Remember that, darlin', in case you get it in a test one day.

If you have might you will fight and blight everything, my lady. Is such for you humans, I know, but do not fear my judgment, for I am gentle tonight, only a messenger travelling across the dark night of this almighty universe. I harm no one on starlit nights. The Lord of Death – but you can call me Skerrit! – is a sound judge in and on all matters. Even when I under them! So I will tell you what I will do. Go on your way, and no thunder shall follow you! Tread softly, find peace and happiness as best you can in this Trinidad, and don't mind is all tatters here and that you may have to go overseas to find peace with a man call Reece! And last but not least, beware the wrath of the Midnight Robber in Trinidad!

Was then I see what paint on the little heads the Midnight Robber had hanging all round the sombrero he wearing. Each head was the size of a egg, maybe a little bigger, and I start to recognize the faces of the politicians of the day – the Prime Minister no less, grinning the grin of a jackass; the Opposition Leader, all white-haired as usual and smiling just like the Madam that morning I hear the birds for the first time. The Attorney General, the Minister of National Security, the Commissioner of Police, the Health Minister – some people does call him Leather Face – and a big man with the banks, a white fellah, and a few others I couldn't recognize. The Robber had paint some of their faces on what look like eggshells, others he had cut out their picture from the newspapers and stick them on the eggshells.

As the Midnight Robber walk away he point a arm up at the sky and shout at the stars, telling them they must behave tonight and shine real bright, because if not, he will fly up there and rearrange them with a backhoe.

I wasn't too 'fraid while the Robber was talking, but as he was walking away he turn and make a pretend dash for me, and I start to run to Saddle Road. I run and run, and I run *fast*, and I sure I lose a five pounds.

A few days pass, and the whole time I 'fraid to go back by Madam, so I don't go. Nobody could call me; Madam eh know what going on, and I couldn't find Madam number anywhere – was only on my cell phone I had it, and since I didn't call she much, I couldn't remember the number. I was 'fraid too bad. I feel them boys coming to look for me, or they get catch and a next one belonging to the gang coming to kill me. I stay by my father. He carry me in the Church and they pray on me, and after a few days pass I start to feel a little better.

When I go back by Madam last Friday afternoon, she vex. Real vex. I give she the hundred dollars she had give me for the sleeping tablets, but she never say thanks. She looking like she hadn't sleep since last I see she, and before I could explain what happen, she ask why I so like all of them other black people it have in Trinidad. Then she start to call me Negro and say, *If we was in the good old Guyana days, I woulda pitch out yuh black ass long time!*

Well, look at my crosses. I never know white people could cuss so like Laventille Old Nigger. And right then and there I tell the woman I hope she catch a pleurisy and *dead*. And we start to cuss, and the Madam bawling how ungrateful black people is, how all we know to do is vote the Jackass Prime Minister back into office, never mind Madam know I never vote for that *fetid obscenity* – them is words my father say once to a man who come by complaining how we mango tree growing over in his yard and we must cut it down because it obstructing his view, and my father, who studying for teacher certificate in them days, open up a big dictionary – *The Chambers English Dictionary* – he had it in his hand then and come out with them two word. The man watch him hard, say my father is not a Trinidadian, and then he spit on the ground and walk away.

A fetid obscenity. It sound powerful – that is real insulting English there, you hear? And was my father Derrick Jones find them two word in the English Language, and lash it out on that ignorant red man living next door. Ever since I first hear them words, I know they just right, they mysterious and magical. I will never forget how the red man look back at we as he walk away after spitting he little spit, like he feel is a curse my father put on him with those educated word.

So, I pose up myself good and proper and watch Old Bitch straight in she loose, dry-up, lonely face, on which I sure more scalpel pass than the General Hospital see in the last year, and I call *she* a fetid obscenity! And just like when you see maxi taxi stop sudden-sudden in the middle of the road to pick up somebody, so Old Bitch freeze when she hear them two word. Was like a revelation pass over Old Bitch face for a few moments, because from the time I say what I say she get stupid as a manicou when light shine in it face at night. Then she catch sheself and start to cuss one set of Devil cuss. At that moment in come the daughter. And she stand up quiet-quiet and watch Old Bitch and me like she *eh even know who we is*. The new, pretty nose she had surgery on last year – like mother like daughter, eh? – turn up as if she does shit ice-cream.

Old Bitch stop cussing when she see how the daughter stand up there watching we. The daughter roll she eye and say, *You all don't know how to behave? The children are awake, Ryan is home trying to sleep because he was on call all last night, and the whole neighbourhood must be wondering what the hell is going on.*

Then she say to Old Bitch, *Where is Sadie? I need help controlling these damn children.*

Old Bitch turn and call for Sadie, and I see a young Coolie come from the kitchen, nice and fresh looking; she must be from South, by Cedros side, because you could see the Venezuelan blood she mix with, the complexion almost as light as Old Bitch own.

Yes, Madam? she say.

Help Mrs. Adamson with those children, please. I'm exhausted talking to this black woman.

Yes, Madam.

The good Coolie girl walk out with a bowed head, if you please. That was when Old Bitch start to smile the same smile the Opposition Leader does smile when something up his sleeve, as if he have gold or cocaine in he backyard. Then is when I realize what really going on. Old Bitch look at me and say in she best Laventille Old Nigger voice, *And she doh thief!*

Give she time, I say, remembering the Opposition Leader. *Give she time. All of we is one in this Trinidad when it come to corruption.*

Look, I not able with the two of you all, Mrs. Adamson say, and she turn on she fancy high-heels and tock-tock out of the apartment.

Get yuh black ass out of this compound, you hear me? Old Bitch say. *Before I call the guard!* And she raise she arm and point a finger upwards, just like the Prime Minister does do when he talking shit in Parliament.

I watch she. *Yes*, I say, *I going. I will call the guard for you, your Majesty.*

She cuss me again.

So I start to walk out through the compound as the sun going down, seeing people looking out their window at me, some of them standing up by their door as if they never see a black woman yet.

And yes, of course I steal Old Bitch cell phone! I take the damn phone home and pitch it down hard and I mash it up fine-fine with the strong, low-heel shoes I was wearing. But I never take nothing else, as God is my Witness. *Yes*, I thief Old Bitch cell phone, because was *over a year* I take she blasted abuse asking me where I put this and that, if I take this or that. And when the daughter begin to accuse me… well! Every day I went by Old Bitch, was like a song in my head.

Cynthia, where my scissors? Cynthia, where my red silk top? Cynthia, have you seen the crystal ashtray? I thought I had four pounds of chicken in the freezer… Damn it, man! Where the bottle of detergent I had on top the washing machine?

And so on and so forth until I *had* was to thief something, in truth.

As I leave Madam place for the last time, I find myself wondering about the Midnight Robber I meet the night after the robbery murder in the pharmacy. As the last sunlight touch the Maraval hills and darkness settle all around, I take a left after the guard hut (the guard was winding he waist as usual, and never even see me leave) and begin the walk through Fairways, avoiding the traffic rush and all the mad-ass Trini it have down by the pharmacy. I wanted to settle myself, and too I was hoping to see the Midnight Robber again, because when you think about it, is only a Midnight Robber could save this Trinidad.

But I never see him.

By the time I reach the centre of Fairways, I look up at the stars, pretty-pretty again in the night sky, and I swear I see a outline of the Midnight Robber riding a backhoe among the stars, with he sombrero and black cape stretching out across the long dark universe.

IN THE CAGE

The man and young woman are standing close together at the jaguar's cage. There is a rail in front of them, six feet from the cage, and they lean on it. The tropical sun is on the jaguar as he lies on his back; they can see the pale fur of his belly and chest. His large front paws are near his heavy jaws, while the top of his head touches the wet concrete floor.

Dusk is appearing; fresh bruises in a pale sky. Most of the visitors have left, and the sun, now filtered by other cages, other trees, and the dust and haze of a late afternoon in the dry season, is golden. They are quite alone, it seems, and feel, in the several acres of cages, almost imperial, as if they can do whatever they wish.

He, watching her watch the jaguar, has his hand around her waist, trying to feel if she has on underwear beneath her loose, knee-length skirt. The jaguar shifts onto his belly and regards them with an eloquent disdain; then he curls down between his legs, his rosette coat celebrating the last sunlight, and begins licking his neatly furred, perfectly round, plump testicles.

She hums. "He's so beautiful. Must be cool after the rinsing."

He agrees.

"Don't you wish you could lick yourself like that?"

He moves around to lean against her back, his hand busy between her legs. He grunts.

"Don't you just hate that tomorrow is Monday?" she says, distracted.

It is something she has asked often during the last nine months, but in other places and situations, so he hears the tone of her voice, the way the words fall into order, one after another as if for the first time. Yet he makes no response.

"Well," she says, "*am* I wearing any?"

The tip of his tongue dabs the fine cartilagineous ridges just inside her ear. She sighs; her blonde head falls forward a little, and the wet stickiness of his tongue, the tingling sensation in her ear, arm and neck, undo her. "Come on," she says, her breath quick, "let's do it here."

She is very wet and encourages him by lifting the back of her skirt. He looks around, nervous, but is not about to start saying no – they have never denied one another – and unzips his jeans. She, looking at the jaguar, leans forward a bit more on the rail.

He's thinking of tomorrow, Monday, his job as a boarding clerk with a shipping agency in the ramshackle capital city. Dusk is becoming a fuchsia gash in the sky. He hurries the sex, resenting the work he must attend to on Monday; resenting the predictability of the day to come. Of knowing exactly when he will call her, what they will say, where they'll have lunch, and what the operator who always connects him to her says.

Hold a second, sir, and I'll put you through.

Indeed.

A scent like the sea alerts the jaguar. He looks at the man and woman. The man stares into his eyes.

There was a cargo ship, some five years before, of the kind that runs back and forth along the Caribbean coast of South America, and the jaguar had been on it in a cage. On certain days, there were long bright beaches in the distance. The ship rose and fell on these windy blue days, and when the jaguar wasn't sick, he gazed out across the sea at the beaches.

She looks back at the man, her eyes their brightest blue, and he tries to mask the sadness in his face.

A LANDSCAPE FAR FROM HOME

Smoke left the steamboat's funnel in an unhurried curve, floated above the stern, and then the wake, foamy silver on the river. The only sound was the muffled chug-chug of the engine. Anna and Gene were sweating in the heat – Gene far more – and squinting at the glare. They wore swimsuits and sat in canvas chairs.

"Damn this heat," Gene said. "I swear to God, August gets worse every year." He shifted, flicking sweat off his body. The gold chain around his neck glinted.

"At least we get rain in the afternoons," Anna said. Her voice was soft, melancholy; it went with her dark hair and the long oval of her face. Her eyes, too, were dark, and hinted at the sadness of a long-settled malaise.

She was aware of the boatman, an Amerindian in the corrugated-iron shelter to their right, observing her with a sneer. The cargo, farm produce and lumber, was destined, as they were, for Georgetown, eighty miles away at the mouth of the Demerara.

Anna, in a dark green bikini, tried to settle into her tanning. Had she and Gene been on the Riviera – where they'd gone last summer – she would have tanned nude, and preferably without him there because of his behaviour since being denied promotion at the advertising agency a year ago. But here, heading north to the muddy Atlantic coast of this former colony in South America, recently described in a UN report, according to a journalist in *Vanity Fair*, as a ghetto country, a place where international terrorists held sway, sitting in a bikini made her feel uncomfortable, despite the fact she'd been a model until a few years ago. The effect it was having on the boatman was disturbing – the set of his face when staring at her browned body. She began to wonder if he was familiar with certain magazines and, perhaps, the photographs of her in them.

"Seems like the boatman's seen me before," she said.

Gene grinned easily. "A country like this? I doubt it. He probably can't even read."

"Isn't that somewhat presumptuous?"

"Be happy. We're on holiday."

A boat with ten Amerindians, heading south, was passing by. Remembering one of Gene's stories about his childhood here with his grandfather, stories he'd told her in Toronto to seduce her into coming, Anna expected them to wave, maybe even recognize Gene. But the adults and children, their clothes tattered and loose, stared indifferently at them. Then she became aware of bundles and boxes, ancient suitcases and knapsacks: they were searching for a new home, fleeing the spreading violence in the country. They would have to go far, far south, she knew, remembering another of Gene's stories, one told on their first night at the old family house up-river.

The sun was right above them, but invisible in a haze.

"I can't believe we have five more hours of this," Gene said. "I'll die of dehydration. We should have taken the land route."

"Try and enjoy it," she murmured.

"I don't have an admirer."

"Of course you do."

She made a show of watching him.

There was a small pool of sweat between the rolls of fat on Gene's stomach. He wiped the sweat from his eyes and grimaced as he picked up his sunglasses. She imagined the tinted world he'd see through them and searched for her own sunglasses, darker than his. Through hers the land, air, and river looked cooler, inviting even. But instead of achieving more privacy, she felt more exposed. She glanced at the boatman; he was grinning fatuously. The audacity surprised her: they hadn't been underway two hours, and Gene was beside her.

"He's really staring," she said.

"He's harmless. All he cares about is survival. Getting the owner's boat back safely."

"That's the danger." She sighed.

Gene hummed.

Behind his sunglasses, an expensive pair with frames of tortoise shell, Gene seemed unrecognizable; he possessed the kind of narrow, boyish face – hair tinted silver – whose distinguishing features were easily hidden.

"I'd like to start working again," Anna said.

He turned to her, slid his sunglasses down his nose, and blinked – once, twice. "What kind of work?"

"Something better than before."

"Difficult," he said. "But I can talk to the agency. I may get a little sympathy."

"I mean full time." She watched him carefully.

He gave her his little look again. "Toronto is in recession too, you know." He turned away, tilting his head back. His gold chain was embedded in the wet hair of his chest.

He's oozing comfortably now, she thought.

Gene fidgeted; the excess flesh on his stomach shook, sweat splashed off, fell to the deck, and evaporated almost instantly. A stale scent of his cologne and body odour whiffed by. She wanted rain. The low barrier around the deck hindered the air. The cargo was stacked from the stern to right behind them, so she felt hemmed in. She sat up, and warm air drifted onto her face.

He said, "I suppose this is better than the land trip would have been. Though you can't be sure."

"Of course it is. Healthier too: we're losing weight and getting a tan. What we wanted."

"More like a greasy roast," he said irritably. "And to think I paid El Capitan here exactly what he wanted." Gene looked at him.

El Capitan grinned at them and pointed to the sky. "Rain coming," he said. The words were almost inaudible.

"We should be careful of the sun, even if there are clouds."

"You'd better believe it."

"The clouds may be making it worse. At least it seems like that."

"Damn ozone layer," Gene said. "Or is it the greenhouse effect?"

He sat up. Taller, he could see clearly out over the barrier. She watched him looking at the distant beach and jungle and wondered if he were recollecting his childhood trips here with his grandfather. The stories Gene had told her of that time were too few, and he had stopped telling them altogether because he thought she preferred them to him; preferred the adventurous, fun-loving child he'd been. But this weekend trip from Georgetown to New Amsterdam, then to the old house up-river, formerly owned by Gene's grandfather and now by his cousins, with its dull-red roof and timber from another century, had been alien to her.

"Childhood dreams are lies," he had said on their first night, as they sat on the balcony looking at the lights across the river. "When I was a boy, you could live off the land here, not just crops, but wildlife. My grandfather had planned to do it. Now anyone wanting to live off the land has to travel hundreds of miles up-river." Then he had pointed south through the windows of the great house open to the night.

"Were there really dolphins in this river when you were a boy?" she asked now, in the heat and light of day.

"So my grandfather said. Pale silver, like the moon." He paused. "I think I saw some playing off the beach. Once."

She lay back and closed her eyes.

Pale silver, like the moon. As though the words had come from some long-abandoned part of him. Before shutting her eyes, she'd noticed the unfamiliarity of the emotion of those words on his face. He could have been reacting to the stirrings of a sweet, vague memory that sought to disturb his separation from the time of his childhood at the old house. Gene's childhood had been like no other she'd heard of; he'd spoken about long days on the river fishing with his grandfather, days in which childhood filled the world. She had never experienced such a world.

Gene said, "I see El Capitan has indeed taken something of an interest in you. If I start talking to him, maybe he'll stop staring."

"I wish you would," she said quietly.

"Does it matter?"

She didn't answer. She kept her eyes shut, letting images of a boy and his grandfather strolling along a near golden beach in late afternoon to look for the pug marks of jaguars take hold of her, comfort her. They found none, of course, the big cats having learned to stay away from humans. But later, returning to the house at dusk, the sun striking its red roof ablaze, they would see the dolphins, their bodies the silver of moonlight in the dark water.

Gene, at the bow, adjusted his sunhat. Anna wished he would come to her. Then she wished he wasn't there. The boatman was watching her again. Gene turned, saw this and turned away. Staring at his back, she thought: *Come to me – quickly, before the pleasures of life become extinct. Come to Anna. And fuck her.*

She rose unsteadily, put on a long grey jersey, and went to Gene, still feeling the boatman's eyes on her. She stopped, regarded him, and he sneered appreciatively at her again.

Standing at Gene's side, she saw that they were angling to the right, approaching the mouth of the great river, its shoreline becoming more distinct. The water was choppy. She leaned gently against him and he flinched.

"What if the boatman did something dangerous?" she asked.

"I wouldn't be surprised. Why don't you tan topless? He might become shy." He pulled his sunhat lower.

"Doubtful. But I suppose that would amuse you."

"You know I like to be entertained."

"You're bored," she said plaintively. "Perhaps you're bored with yourself."

"Or maybe with the whole damn world. Tan for us."

She managed a small laugh. "He could kill you, rape me and take our money."

"Now there's excitement, there's risk," he said, nearly smiling.

Land strewn with stumps, razed earth and secondary vegetation became visible. Blue-grey smoke rose straight to a sky the colour of ash. The river was becoming a muddy brown. She noticed, in the silence between Gene and herself, the almost imperceptible rocking of the boat from long, low swells gently flowing from the sea. The land far beyond the riverbank seemed even flatter, without any real jungle; only scatterings of trees remained. It was mottled, scrubby land, the colours of a faded tortoise shell that had been scorched in the sun. The massive expanse of flatness and the great pall of sky gave her the uncanny feeling she was on top of the world and about to fall off, but upward, into the grey ash.

The boatman cleared his throat and spat.

She wanted rain.

She wrapped herself in the loose folds of the jersey and stared down at the brackish water. Gene went back to the sun-chairs, absurd now in the setting – boat chugging along a forgotten river in South America; dying jungle on both sides – and sat down. His presence, sunhat askew, brief swimsuit tight on his plump legs, with the stacks of produce behind the chair, added to the absurdity. She turned her attention back to the water.

An hour passed.

Then another.

Beyond the river and the river's mouth, beyond the scabrous land and ailing huts and houses perched along the beach, she saw fresh clouds against the blue sky, just above the blue line of horizon of the Atlantic. The distance before her subdued her anger at Gene a little, seemed to offer a faint promise of some change soon to come.

The boat rolled and splashed on entering the Atlantic. Gene was asleep on his chair, a towel over his face. The sea breeze ruffled her hair and jersey. In the distance and above, the clouds grew taller, became dull-silvered spirals and toppings of cumulus with large, bloated and rumbling bases. Much of the sea darkened, but they motored through patches of sunlight, the sea here the colour of pale milk chocolate.

They were an hour from Georgetown when the rain started. Gene scrambled beneath the shelter of the boat, forced, finally, to confront the boatman. She stayed out in the rain, further sealing herself off from them. The coastline disappeared in grey mist; steam rose off the deck; the air became cool. The rain soothed her hot scalp, her skin; she wanted to strip, bathe in its wet, grey density. The voices of Gene and the boatman, subdued into murmurs by the rain, soothed her at first; but then, by their very continuity, which suggested a kind of peace she was not part of, she grew to hate the sound. There, in the warm rain soaking through her clothing, she began to wonder if she'd ever loved Gene.

As the low, rust-coloured buildings of Georgetown came into view, she decided she would leave him when they arrived in

Toronto. The destruction was necessary. She must cut him off. Be resolute.

By the time they disembarked in bright, late-afternoon light, the rainstorm over and glistening on the dockyard and jetties, Gene was relating the boatman's history – a series of misadventures and adventures throughout the river network of the country. He'd forgotten their tension, his hurtful words.

When he went to find a taxi, she stood and watched the boatman unloading the portable goods from the boat. The lumber would be lifted off with forklifts later. Not once did he look at her. He was concentrating on carefully placing, lest he dent them, the boxes of tender fruits and vegetables on the jetty.

In the taxi going to Gene's cousin's house, from where they would be driven to the airport in two days time for the flight to Toronto, Gene put his arm around her. She flinched. Passing dilapidated houses of wood, and office buildings in disrepair; passing Amerindians selling multicoloured trinkets, baskets, and carvings; passing open-air markets with the stench of last week's discarded produce, and seeing children empty-faced and moist-eyed begging for food and money, she thought her decision had been made in haste, and that Toronto, that soon-to-be-cool city far to the north, had its own problems.

She eased back on the soft, plastic-covered seat and relaxed a bit. Gene haggled with the driver for a lower price.

She thought: I can wait.

CARIBBEAN HONEYMOON

It is a hot, late afternoon and the young woman and man are being driven through the city, near the sea, past the financial district. The squat concrete buildings – banks, lawyers' offices, and insurance companies – shade the car intermittently, but offer no relief from the heat. The car, rattling like a rusty tambourine, soon passes former colonial homes with high ceilings and pointed roofs, many of them now quaint restaurants with large windows. Their newly painted interiors, peach and lime-green cool, are crowded with customers. Waiters move quickly about, serving the executives and lawyers clusters of ice-cold bottled beer.

They are moving through hotter air, in the oldest part of the city now. Motorists shout and blow their horns at the bullying tactics of their driver; luxury cars careen out of his way. They pass dark bronze statues of political leaders and calypso singers, the leaders with dull faces, blank eyes that seem to indicate their attitude while in power.

The young woman, sitting away from her companion, a man maybe ten years older, feels the grit in the air sticking to her pale skin. She fidgets, attentive to the handbag on her lap. Her hazel eyes are large, sad, she has heavy eyebrows, and her hair hangs in dark-red, clumpy curls. She takes a small hand mirror from her handbag, checks her full lips, her nose, and wipes her cheeks and nose with a folded tissue.

"You look fine," her companion says. "Beautiful. As always."

He watches the back of the driver's neck: the muscles flex to a calypso beat on the car radio.

> *Oh God! Poverty is hell,*
> *But don't mind – don't mind the smell,*
> *Cause everything – everything after here*
> *Is wine and shine, and is only sweet music you will hear!*

She gazes out the window at the distant scattering of slums, in the last light, on the mountains rising directly behind the city. To the west of these, on other mountains – their green lawns discernible even from this distance – are luxury houses.

It is remarkable, she thinks. Everyone has a view.

She longs for rain. Its heavy wetness will cleanse the air and drown the sounds of the city traffic. Perhaps it'll erase, for a short while, her time and place. They are both something she can taste: car exhaust mixing with the dead salt of dirty sea water, the burning of the island, and scent of its dry earth and trees reaching them all the way from the mountains, borne on wind like a reminder of what once was, of a time before fire.

History has brought her here, that and bad decisions: she looks over at one now: he's tapping his fingers on his knee, his hawkish face uneasy, or is it anticipation? He's still watching the back of the driver's head. The driver gestures now and then emphatically, left hand out of the window; sometimes he gets an obscene response. She swallows, feeling tiny grains make their way down her throat. She thinks of cold mountain streams; thinks of lying naked in them, drinking the water through her skin, while watching the cool, green sway of trees above.

On the mountains, as the light fades, little dabs of orange flame become visible. With night, as on so many other nights during the first months of each year, the fires appear floating in the sky, like huge amber necklaces.

They stop at the port, at the ferry service that connects the island with another in the north. The taxi-driver, thinking they are tourists, tries to overcharge them. She glances at her male companion, brushes her hair out of her eyes and says to the driver, "Think we stupid, or what? Just because we white, you think we not from here."

The driver, a black man in his early thirties, says, "Eh-eh, hear she, Mistah. *Hear* she. And like she know the talk, too! I sure she could real pretty up my life. How much you want to give me, darlin'? How much?"

The driver has shifted around in his seat and is looking at them with an almost demented enthusiasm. Now they see he's drunk. He grins.

Her companion leans forward and drops a blue bill on the seat beside the driver. "There," he says casually.

"Tell Glen to improve the transport," she says.

He nods.

The driver removes the money and ignores them now, his little show over. They get out, taking two carry-on bags with them. Walking towards the boarding station, beyond which the massive bulk of the ferry looms, she smells diesel and, stronger here, the dead salt of the sea. Inside, standing in line, she begins to look around. The dull yellow lights, heat, and the scent now of sweat: she has a strong desire to leave everything within her vision; to levitate through and above the station, above the port into the grey, ash-scented air, and beyond it.

There are some tourists, mostly middle-aged and tired. A Mediterranean-looking man, wearing beige trousers and a light cotton shirt, about fifty and alone, joins the line opposite. The other passengers are moving toward either side of a check-in counter. They take up similar positions, and begin to speak quietly.

"How about him?" he asks her, giving a brief nod at the man in the light cotton shirt. "Seems pleasant enough."

"Sure," she says, with a smooth indifference. "Nice and fat."

He says nothing. Then: "He's a tourist."

She looks back at the Mediterranean man.

"We'll get there near midnight, like always," he says. "Then we'll just go straight to Glen's house. Nothing to worry about."

He is staring at the man.

"House. Sounds so funny – no, strange – to be talking like this. You'd think we owned one. A *house*."

"We'll have enough for one soon, well, a condo at least. But forget that," he says. "Think about him."

She thanks him for his advice.

"Stop it," he says.

Their tickets are stamped and torn by a sullen black woman at the check-in counter. Then they notice the Mediterranean man in the cotton shirt has disappeared.

She smiles. "You'll have to find someone else, my dear."

He watches her, irritated.

They board the vessel in silence. The dock lights and city lights brighten further as night deepens. On the sea the darkness has gathered massively, but for now, on the aft deck, they watch it give full life to the vast necklaces of amber fires in the mountains.

"It's so beautiful," she says.

He notices the colour of the fires shows tints not unlike those in her hair, in certain light: an orange-brown gold, like the blaze of hazy sunsets.

They are sitting near the stern.

"What do you think of that one?" he says.

"Where?" She turns away from the island.

"Leaning on the rail, to our left."

She stands up. "He seems okay. But chubby again. You like them like that, don't you?"

"We've done well so far."

"Of course, my dear," she says, doing a little skip and dance three-step. "And so much depends on the ability of my pussy. Pussy power," she says, with a giggle. Then: "Damn thing's itching. I shaved too closely."

"Stop it," he hisses. "He looks suitable."

But she retains the tone. "I feel so close to you at moments like this, darling. But why must they always be near middle-aged and porky? Get me a nice, young buck. Someone who can fuck me silly."

He doesn't reply. She watches his face, as if expecting something. The ferry begins to move; there are vibrations along the railing. The island begins to shift, slipping. The second man moves away. Soon, the scent of decay and fire begins to lessen; there is a light breeze. The sea and night become attractive to look into. She tries to find stars, but he says she has to wait until they are far away from land.

In the rest-room, handbag slung over her shoulder, she examines her face carefully, applies a rich flesh-tone lipstick, and lines her eyes lightly with black mascara. The ferry engine tremors everything: the greasy pipes, the soles of her shoes (from where it travels up her legs, to the tips of her fingers, to the lipstick on her lips), the cling of her blouse, jeans, even the gold chain around her neck.

She leans over the sink closer to the mirror, but its age – cracks, spots, dust, signatures of neglect – distorts her image, so she steps back. She angles her position to the mirror, and there, in the slant of clinical white light, she sees the inner place, that closest part of herself known only to her, nesting in her eyes.

Transfixed by her own stare, she lifts the chain and closes her hand over the medal. She keeps looking at her eyes and visualizes the miniature image, on one side of the medal, of a dolphin leaping and an island with a single palm tree in the background. On the other side are the words: "Toward a State of Grace."

It is from him.

Ab imo pectore.

Outside, at the starboard railing, she rests her elbows on the cool iron: *Young Woman, Alone at Sea. Night*. The darkness of the sea is physical: the wind has texture, moist salt on her cheeks a constant anointing; and its sound is melancholy, whip-whistling shrilly around the rails.

They will cease these activities soon, he's told her. There is nearly enough money. And yes, we can get out. Glen knows he needs new recruits; we've become a little too familiar round here… No, I don't think he'll relocate us. We've done our time, been to the places, seen the sights, and been seen.

She thinks: What about the other thing?

Later she says to him, "Life is madness." She gestures at the wake, now the colour of starlight. "Yet you have this marvellous way of sorting everything out. You're a great organizer, you know; so creative. You should be in government."

"I suppose I could get involved, but it's dirtier than this. We'll certainly have enough money soon. It could be a good investment."

"Is Glen connected?"

He shrugs.

The Mediterranean-looking man they first saw on the dock reappears. He sits down on a bench near one of the sealed, elevated lifeboats, loosens his tie, and begins smoking.

"Look. He's waiting."

She turns around. "The porky man is back," she says. "I like it when they come. They quiver all over, like doves."

She starts across.

"Be careful," he says.

Animula vagula –

"He's an original: actually said no thank you. Told me he was happily married. Told him I was too – almost – but that you had a low sperm count and needed assistance. He seemed to believe that more than an offer of a good fuck."

"Sure he said no? He's looking over. See?"

She ignores him. "I can't wait to get to the house."

"I want you to go back."

"Not interested. I told you."

He appears to consider this for a moment.

"Okay, okay," she says. "Maybe he's surprised by my race. Nice middle-class girl fucking for fun. He must be very traditional, my love. A nice brown-skin might suit him. Oh… he's smiling now. Cute, isn't he? I wonder if he coos."

"Once he knows you're for real –"

"You seem to forget, darling, I'm a nice, university-educated girl who was once very –"

He grabs her arm. "Serena."

"You need me to do it, don't you?"

They are close, looking straight into each other's eyes, her face well below his. They remain that way, for about fifteen seconds.

She backs away from him. For a few moments, she seems sad. But then: "Yes, my love," and does her little three-step routine again.

"Go."

"Are *we* okay?" Her eyes have narrowed, the soft delicate skin around them tensing.

"Don't worry about that. Just enjoy it."

"Don't you like to watch anymore? Or ask about it? You used to. Or do you just imagine it now?"

"I can't always look. It's too risky."

"You're such a funny man."

He waves her away. She goes, leaving him with both of the bags.

For about an hour he watches the dark sea. The wind and gentle sway of the ferry relax him. The island is lost to sight. He checks his watch, yawns, and glances upward. There, cast in a density he has never seen before, are all the stars anyone can imagine. Meteors occasionally cross the blackness.

He remembers a time he enjoyed it so much that the heat from it made him dry-mouthed and he needed water or a beer, preferably a beer – any alcohol, frankly, was better in the beginning. What was it then? It was exquisite sweet pain burning in his heart and chest so much that after they played and he slept beside her, he felt filled with all of the world: nothing could hurt him. Yet it never lasted. He burned to know she'd done it again, and as it went on his thirst grew and he drank more water during that time than ever before.

But it's something else now, has been for a while, and he's curious.

She's standing thirty feet away, leaning on a rail and looking out to sea. The stern light shows the curve of her face; her full-lipped mouth is solemn. He notices her hair: most of it is now held back; gold-red wisps play around her neck. As he moves towards her, she shifts a little, and then straightens.

"Trouble?"

He steps to her, close, is about to embrace her with his left arm around her shoulder when she moves away. He stops. Draws back.

When she turns to him, her eyes reveal nothing. "No. He was quite tickled by it all."

"Nice."

"No problem," she says, trying to reclaim her earlier energy. "There's never any problem, usually… Can we stay longer at the house?"

"Glen won't mind."

He reaches out for her hand, but she doesn't want him to touch her.

The wind is steady, cool and moist, and they listen to it.

★

It is morning and they are in the house. For a few moments, if she closes her eyes, she can imagine it's her place, and there is no Glen or he. In the bedroom upstairs she leaves the curtains open for light and sleeps fitfully for most of the day, sometimes staring out at the blue sea and the thinner blue of the sky. Her companion sleeps in another room, downstairs.

Late in the evening, Glen arrives. He checks the weight and packaging of the parcels they've brought in the carry-on bags. Then they all have drinks.

Glen sits with his legs up on the couch in the living room that gives a view of the sea through a huge glass window behind him. He looks at her with casual lust. The dark sea, from the height of the house on the hill, seems larger than the sky.

"Glen," she says. "Are you with the government?"

Her companion looks over at her instantly.

Glen smiles and lifts his drink. The light from the lamp-table beside the couch glints the crystal glass of scotch as he says, "Darling, I am the government – part of it, anyway."

He is a friendly looking man, a bit portly, older than her companion, and his hair is greying in tufts around his ears. When he tilts his head back and gulps the drink, she sees the lump of his larynx jumping like the beating of a little heart.

FIRE IN THE CITY

Sometimes, when things real quiet in the hills, and it have a nice little breeze so I can't hear Mervyn in the kitchen at the dishes, I does sit in the balcony and watch the lights in town. On such a sweet night, a man just want to cool his brains and think 'bout life, and count his lucky stars he not dead in a violent robbery or something so. People getting shoot and kill all 'bout the place these days. Ever since the government let out them fellahs who try to take over the country some years ago, people feel they could do anything in this island. And they doing it, too. As if they have written authority from the Almighty 'self.

The Mount Hope Correctional Institute for Boys have a real pretty view at night. Lately, I sitting here plenty, almost every night now, like a man possess. Mervyn say he hear some gang want to burn down the city. Is what Mervyn hoping to see, yes, for he tell me is the onliest thing that would set this island right.

Life is a funny thing. Because look how I and Mervyn end up here, minding ten vagrant children (from five to seventeen years), two man with responsibility and a little money in the bank every month from the Organization of Catholics for Reconstructive Action.

So how I get here? Was a bacchanal night like all them other nights. I and my friend Aucks, Auckinson Stewart, Trini man-'bout-town and so-call car-mechanic genius, went Parliament Bar, the best place for drinking and woman I did know 'bout then. Sometimes Aucks would be waiting for me with a cold beer in his hand outside Parliament, which wasn't far from where I was living then. Aucks did always know a bartender there, and from the time I finish a beer or rum, was a next one in my hand. No skylarking with fete in them days, you understand. We would warm up weself in Parliament, discussin' where we going and what we go do, before ridin' out into the night.

In them days, my parents know I home only when I wake up at midday and eating breakfast. My mother did always say something like, *But eh eh – Nello! You turning Dracula?* Then Pops would come out with he face all dry up from rum, shuffling the newspapers, and when he see me, grunt like a man who vote PNM all he life, have diabetes and can't get proper health care. Then my small sister, Janelle, eyes pretty like the lights I seeing from the hills – she did always jump up and down 'til I hug she.

I never get much education. Since from small I was cleaning somebody yard, washing car, whatever it have – but I did always know how to treat my family good. Up to now my mother still sending food for me here, but I tell she long time now no need for that. Mervyn could cook a good stew when he ready. I was always bringing present for Janelle and my mother in them days, yes. Except for Pops, and all the rum he was drinking, life was sweet.

Then things change when the whole island hit hard times and I had was to run round mad-ass Port of Spain looking for work. And wasn't only Trinidad, was the whole Caribbean, and America too what get hit with recession. What a man like me supposed to do? Was only car parts Aucks and I was stealing – just enough to get decent food, clothes and have a little fun now and again. Pops trouble was he could never understand that, yes. I didn't beat nobody, I didn't kill nobody.

If wasn't for Pops and all he complaining, them days with my family could have be even better. As if was *he* paying for Janelle schooling. He did grow up in them days when penny was worth penny, so he could never accept the easy money I was getting – coming home with all them gifts, and too besides, supporting Janelle. Drinking rum was the onliest thing that man ever learn how to do without help.

So, was a bacchanal night like all them other nights, as I tell you. Aucks and I went Parliament, and from there the Garden of Eden.

Aucks had the latest in them Japanese executive car – everything automatic, everywhere air-condition; he *have* to be the coolest man in town. The car had sound-system, alarm and a little black pager attach to his keys so he could know when thief thiefing. Beep! Beep! it uses to go, as if he was a big-time doctor or something. But as far as I could tell, car and woman was the onliest thing Aucks was doctoring. Aucks did real like to speed and play kaiso in the car, always showing off the sound-system, like he invent the blasted thing. But it uses to sound wicked sweet, I not going to lie. And them pothole (Trinidad road *make* with pothole) I was hardly feeling, because Aucks had own a mechanic shop, so the shocks was working *real* good. As usual, it had a cooler of beers in the back seat, and I was sucking the second one by the time we hit Parliament. And man, hear nuh, that night I was feeling like my whole life now start. Compare to what I was getting before, the money from the car parts business flowing like water in the rainy season. Still, I should have know better.

When Aucks and I pull up in Parliament car park, Aucks say, *Nello, boy! We reach!* And he slap me on my back – hard – so it sting. *How it feeling to be in Paradise, Nello?*

He was always asking me thing like that, especially on a Friday night, playing up as if I should always be so focking humble and grateful that is because of *he* I had good money. In truth, was no set of big money I was making with Aucks, but no real hardship was involve in the work. I uses to cruise round in them days when car alarm wasn't so fancy and pick a car, and the two fellers in the back seat of the beat-up Datsun 180B Aucks lend me (right, yes, he was helpful, but was his father who own the business, so in truth Aucks wasn't any different than most of the young fellers it have in this damn island: he just slip into Daddy shoes; he play it safe, he go by the money. Maybe is a smart thing, because the island have so little opportunity, but still, putting on Daddy shoes don't make a real man); anyway them two fellers in the back of the 180B – I sure they dead by now – would hop out and in minutes, while I keeping watch, they in a next car. Then quiet and cool we drive off. That was the best way to move, not like these vagrant boys today running round in packs like wild dog looking as if they go take the clothes off your back – or worse, kill you. The best thing is to move like the people you want to thief from. I hear that is what them politicians and big-business boys doing these days.

It have a professor feller, a Indian, who writing in the papers midweek, and this man making them big-time politician thief in their Armani suit look real jackass ignorant, yes. So much corruption and bacchanal he exposing is a wonder they ain't kill him yet. But is not all the time I can read this feller easy, because sometimes he does have to be a professor and write in the normal English and thing, 'bout book and what the politicians doing and not doing, but when he writing in we island English, when he pretending to be a feller like me, like how I talking here, I could follow most times. He write about a feller call CC (Concern Citizen) in the island English, and does end the story with CC asking, *What we go do? What we go do?* And this question start playing in my head like a calypso that stick, and my name does fall into the questions, and start to move around, like the professor want his words dancing up in *my* brains like a crowd on J'Ouvert Morning, trying to get me to answer the question!

Nello, what we go do? Man, Nello, look, what it have to do here? What we go do? Nello, is time to go do something before the gang Mervyn talk 'bout burn down the whole blasted city.

You hear?

But back to Aucks: he was only trying to make me feel good with all the Paradise talk. I didn't really mind his company. People did like to be seen with him, so I didn't really mind the bossy treatment he would get on with now and again. He was a sharp dresser, shoes was always shine and his pants and shirt iron like new. I had never know anyone who dress like a gentleman.

Parliament have a set of old anchor, license plate, rope, net and faded picture up on the walls and roof beams, and some of these decoration does go way back to the 1950s. One time Aucks tell me more alcoholics make in Parliament than anywhere else in the whole island. You could put money on it, he say. When you go in, the door does bang behind you loud-loud – like the Potogee owner deaf or something because for years it banging so. The floor red with square tile and it have a quieter place on the left – with a bar too – for people who want to sit close and talk or watch TV. Aucks and I did only go to that part if it had woman, or if the bar by the entrance was crowded.

That night, as usual, the smell of pee hit we hard outside the entrance. Aucks uses to say the owner leaving it there because it does make people liming outside the door come in, and when they in, is more drinks they going to buy. But in truth, Trinidad people so desperate to have somewhere to go that the Potogee didn't have to strategize 'bout no pee. Pee or no pee, Trinis will fete in a cardboard box if it have nowhere else.

On the other side of the bar by the entrance it have a small game room, and past that, a dartboard that mostly older men uses to prick – when they couldn't prick nothing else, according to Aucks. I remember it had some nice Marley playing the night we arrive. Was "Redemption Song".

Mervyn could real bang dish in a kitchen, yes, like maybe the night too quiet for him. But since he start losing weight and getting sick, he more careless. The boys seeing it too: they know he can't catch them fast like before if they misbehave. They wearing him down these days. If you ask me, is best to give them each a little cough mixture from the medicine cabinet with dinner, so by 7:30 they all asleep. Then I and Mervyn could chill here, take in the lights for a couple hours extra, and talk man to man.

Apart from Benny, Thomas, Gerald and Dirk, the boys well behave. Is ten of them we have here. I and Mervyn sometimes have to put some lash on Benny and Dirk, as too often they trying to bully the other boys, and they like to encourage Thomas and Gerald in all kind of slackness. Thomas and Gerald going along cool-cool, no questions, like is the thing to do. Plenty time we catch them stealing food send to the Institute by the little family some of the boys still have remaining in this world. Like they learning to be politician from small. Is what I does think 'bout when I putting some good lash on their backside.

I and Mervyn have to watch the boys, keep the place clean and cook some food. Brother Michael Jones and Sister Maureen Bennett come by regular to check on us, and we have to attend the religious teachings. Is a big old rundown house we living in, sitting on top a mountain in the northern part of the island, with trees and bush all round. It have a lawn in the back by a cliff reaching up to more trees, and the cliff earth have a colour like gold in the afternoon, when it sunny. Except for firearms discharging in the distance a few times a week, round here quiet.

Is not a bad work, really – I get lucky, I have to say. We does get to watch movies on a video somebody donate to the Institute, but mostly is old Westerns, because Sister Maureen and Brother Michael don't like anything too fancy. It can't have naked woman, bad language or too much tenderness. And the bad fellers must get shoot good and dead by the end, or else.

When the police arrest me, the Organization of Catholics for Reconstructive Action challenge the jail sentence, saying it have too much harden criminal in jail, and that I would come out much worse than I went in. I don't know how them holy people swing that one, but talk is that things in the island so bad a few of them powerful enough get together and start to wheel and deal with the government and law officers. Must be guilt, yes. You know how many people die because they make a jail in this mad-ass island? Is either they get kill in jail, or beat up and sick, like Mervyn. They send Mervyn in jail for taking two frozen chicken from the grocery, and the only reason they catch him was because Mervyn was so hungry he had to stop and eat the damn chicken, hiding in somebody yard and sucking bone like a stray dog. The lady who living there was watering her garden and bawl, *Thief! Thief!* when she see Mervyn. Then she start to wet down poor Mervyn with the hose. Next thing, police ride up in a car from the grocery and see him trying to run away, soaking wet and eating a raw chicken. Mervyn say even while he was running he chewing chicken and thinking, *Look at where Mankind reach! Look at where I going,* and when police hold him, he still eating. But the best thing, Mervyn say, was the police let him finish eat the chicken. The other one the police give back to the Chinee lady who own the grocery Mervyn thief from. I doubt she keep it. But you never know, eh, people love money too much in this island. And Chinee people not easy.

"Mervyn!"

Is time he come outside and lime, yes. Last week he fall down inside that hot kitchen. But I know he, he go take his cool time.

In Parliament now, Aucks lean up on the bar, but he can't see no barman or barwoman he know. And the short bald-head Potogee owner look as if he doing us a favour by coming over quick-quick. Aucks watch him hard and tell him to bring two beers. Before, 'bout a year ago, Aucks and he had nearly get in fight – over woman. Aucks was always brushing he eye on girl, even if she have man. So now the Potogee bang the beers down. The beers froth up and spill on the counter. He looking at Aucks and me like he straining, trying to remember *who* we is.

Aucks, vex with how the Potogee serve the beers, say, *Like I know your mother, or what?*

Well. The Potogee suck he teeth and watch Aucks hard like that was the worse thing Aucks could have say. But he only shake his head and went to a next customer. Aucks was a feller I did know long time then, as I say, and he didn't take hard stare from *no* man. If you was a man and not Aucks friend, you could be somebody to beat. No lie.

Now, since Aucks and I come in Parliament, we check out the place. Is woman I talking 'bout. A lady was brushing up against a wall, like she trying to cool she self down. I thinking, *Soon, when the time right, we go start chatting she up.* And in truth, that was all I had hope for that night. But look at how my life change, eh.

Ten dollars.

Was the Potogee. He want cash for the beers.

Open a account, Aucks say.

The Potogee say Aucks don't have that privilege again.

Aucks whisper something 'bout his mother, to no one in particular. Then I see the Potogee face get red-red. Next thing, he spring over the bar like a kangaroo and – blats! – his two thick, strong foot hit the ground.

I say, *Aucks, you sure you want to fight he?* The Potogee looking real strong, arms and them big and hard like he was lifting plenty iron and thing since last we see him. But Aucks like he can't hear, he vex, he ready to fight.

Is so man in Trinidad is.

You say something about my mother? the Potogee ask.

Why I can't have a account here? Aucks ask.

Because I say so – I am the boss.

Like you want to be a dead boss, Aucks say, and break his beer bottle on the counter.

Trouble start then. The Potogee rush Aucks, Aucks cut he face and the Potogee knock Aucks up against a wall. The wind left

Aucks and his face get a funny colour, like it want to be blue. From the time the Potogee see blood on his shirt, he say he going to kill Aucks, that Aucks going to meet his maker now in Parliament, so he better take a good last look round the place. I see Aucks shake he head. The Potogee push me aside and I say, *When you want me Aucks, when you want me!*

As if I could fight! I never was a fighter, in truth, was only style I uses to make. Aucks rush the Potogee, who bring his knee up as Aucks butt him in the belly. A girl scream now she realise is true-true fight. The beer on the ground make Aucks slip, the Potogee slip – brataks! – they fall down. They scramble up, the Potogee grab a chair and throw it at Aucks and Aucks hit it away and it fly onto a girl backside. A good thing she was packing something there, yes.

Then they wrestling: Aucks have a forearm lock up round the Potogee neck; the Potogee face get more red, like he get instant sunburn. The Potogee eye start to bulge out his head and he start to wriggle up on the ground, like he doing some new Carnival dance. He grab Aucks' balls, so Aucks did have no choice but to let go. They both scramble up and the Potogee pull out a knife. The girl scream again, like she realise is murder now. Somebody shout, *Call the police!* Somebody else say they coming already. Aucks and the Potogee face each other, breathing real hard.

Come! Aucks say.

But the Potogee like he get stupid, or something. From the time he hear the word police, he thinking real hard, as if police going to break down the door any second.

Too much fockin' fight! somebody yell, and the Potogee cock he head. Then I know police warn him 'bout fight before. Then somebody else yell, *All-you go from here! Is all man who fighting getting in trouble. Go!*

And the feller who say that, like he know what he was talking 'bout. The man had some serious scar on his face.

I watch Aucks. *Nello,* he say, *the night too young. Let we go from here.*

Man, we leave that place *fast*, not even thinking how people know it had police coming. We screech out the car park like fellers in a detective show, and next thing we tearing through Port of Spain doing seventy-something. The streets was in flashback.

Hear nuh, man, in some ways it was a sweet life I had going then, yes. But when it did come to driving, Aucks wasn't easy. He wasn't easy at all at all. He felt he was boss on the road. Once Aucks overtake ten cars in a row and then swerve round a corner and nearly hit a bus head on. It was wild and stupid to drive so, yes, and when I think 'bout the number of people getting kill in car accident every month in this island now, I want to bawl.

In five minutes we pull into a mall. Aucks start to cuss. He pull a cloth from the glove compartment, reach in the back in the cooler to wet the cloth, and begin to wipe his face and arm. Then he take off his shirt, pants, he clean he shoes, he reach in the back again and get a fresh shirt and pants and a comb. He open two more beers, give me one. The man did have style. And then we gone – we lose that mall, making tracks to the Garden of Eden, where the real action was happening.

Like Mervyn don't want to come outside.

"Jumbie hold you, Mervyn? When you come, make sure you bring the jumbie in the bottle, you hear?"

I wonder if he remember where we hide the rum. The boys and them getting too bold these days, we have to watch them good, and they just at the age where they looking to drink and do God know what else. Boys is boys, no matter where you go, but the ones we have here is a special type. From the time they get to know you a little bit, they make you think they is your friend, then they playing your head. If wasn't for Sister Maureen and Brother Michael, I and Mervyn couldn't manage: the boys like they 'fraid them. Is a hold they have on Mervyn, too, and like the more sick Mervyn getting, the more Brother Michael and Sister Maureen saying he must convert to Catholic. But Mervyn say his mother go dead if he stop being Baptist. Yet still Brother Michael and Sister Maureen trying to make the man change his mind.

I and Mervyn have nowhere to go. When Mervyn start to get sick by his parents' house – that was where he gone after he come out of jail – his father throw him out and Mervyn end up at the Mount Hope Correctional Institute for Boys. When Pops' liver kill him, my mother and Janelle travel to South to live with the family on my mother side; the hospital clean she out of house and home with the money for Pops' medicine and room. Over forty years this government promising to improve the Health Service – and with all the gas and oil money it have in this mad-ass island, you know the jackasses could do it if they really want. But not them, they like to see black people suffer and bawl 'bout how it have a *parasitic oligarchy* what bleeding the wealth of the island. Then the government gone and build new airport and thief millions of taxpayer dollars – in front taxpayer face. And what taxpayer do? Not a damn, blasted thing. But that is how Trinidad is, yes. Sometimes I feel Mervyn right 'bout hoping the whole of Port of Spain get burn down, because this place too corrupt. People only want to fill their pocket with cash and drive fancy car. Like I say, was overnight this island change – a set of people get real rich, and then a bigger set of people get dirt-licking poor. And so it going on, with no end in sight.

The longer I and Mervyn stay here the more dependent we getting on the Catholic assistance. But don't get me wrong, hear, the boys is good boys mostly, we like them plenty, is just that if anything happen to them or the house, I and Mervyn have Hell to answer to. You get where I coming from? The Catholics save us from jail – well not Mervyn, but at least they get him out to live the rest of his life comfortable – so they expecting a little something in return. I don't mind that so much, is just that it could be a little better if we wasn't getting a whole set of religious teachings every Sunday morning. If they was using the Good Book to help we to read better, I wouldn't mind, for it have a set of old book, some with picture on the cover that really make me want know the story, in a library downstairs, but try all I try, I can't catch the story in them books. After a few pages, my head tired.

The house and the library uses to belong to a old Irish feller who come out here 'bout a hundred years ago; Sister Maureen tell me he was a very educated man with money and *a passion for reading*. One afternoon Sister and me was in the library, the boys was playing cricket at the back of the house with Mervyn and Brother Michael, and Sister look up at all them book reaching up to the ceiling and all across a long high wall, and she say, *You know, Nello, there is only one book, and everything comes from it. And that book is the Holy Bible.*

103

Well, right there I know I wasn't going to learn how to improve my reading except to hear every Sunday morning what in the Good Book, as Brother Michael and Sister Maureen call it. But I say, *Sister, if I was that Irishman, I would find a way to come back to the whole world, be everywhere one time, because the world have plenty more book than what here, not so?*

She watch me hard.

But I not finish my story. Aucks and me was flying real low over the highway by the sea, the sea big and dark like a mystery world, a world that don't know what going on in this island. Passing on the highway that night I did watch all them small, wood house on the hills, plenty with fire light, wondering how people who fighting to full their belly four years ago was making out today. Is only two ways to fix that problem – and even if they could get a work, often times it don't pay enough – so is crime they getting involve in. And if you feel nobody have a right to do that, that there always something else to do, I say no, you wrong, maybe it was so ten years ago, but now things *very* different, now things off balance. You understand? You know that Tracy Chapman song "Talking 'bout World Revolution"? You must remember it. And I not saying mankind must rise up and burn down the city like Mervyn say he hear the gang want to do, or make blood flow in the streets, like that revolution they had in France. Brother Michael tell me and Mervyn 'bout that. Heads bounce in the streets, Brother Michael say, like vulture jumping up by the Beetham Highway rubbish dump. And he say was a good thing! In truth, these Catholics could be real nice, but sometimes they *real* hard to understand, yes. Sometimes, is like they trying hard not to think much 'bout the world. Plenty time I hear Sister Maureen say, *It is God's will, it is all a part of God's plan, Nello, and you mustn't question it. Only He knows what He is doing.* That kind of talk does real frighten me, yes, especially when mankind boldface shooting away all kind of people in this island. Is as if Sister giving up on the life that all round us, the life we could see and touch and feel, to believe in something she can't see, touch or feel. Don't get me wrong, eh, I believe in God. Is just that these Catholics does go 'bout believing in a funny way. Is like they denying – they always telling I, Mervyn and the boys to deny deny deny – the life here for the one to come. *If* it coming. Is the same with them Muslims. And the worse things get, is like the more contented these Catholics get, as if this God planning all this madness in truth and they must love him for it. It don't make sense, I tell you. Especially when you think 'bout how God make this world, a world that I know, because I could still remember and even see it from here in the hills at night, have so much beauty in it that it does make me wonder how the Catholics could say He make it in seven days! Brother Michael tell me that, and Sister too, and I say, *Maybe the Bible mean seven million years? Because if the world have so much beauty in it, how He could do it so fast?* But they set up their face and say, *He can do anything.* And then is when I start to think, *Well, if He make it so damn fast, He don't really care.*

But such things wasn't in my head that night Aucks and I riding out to the Garden of Eden. Now, looking back, I see everything clear-clear, and I always kicking myself that I didn't notice what Aucks was really doing with Selwyn. This man Selwyn think he too is God gift to all woman from Eve come forward. Both of them was smart-man trying to outdo the other. But I didn't know then.

I know now.

So there we was, cruising through the night, driving along that coast that always so nice on moonlit night, seeing all the way down to the bauxite station, even to the prison island.

When we hit Garden of Eden, it jam-pack. I never see that place so pack yet. And woman. If you did see woman – all kind of woman. It had Chinee and Indian woman, White woman and Black woman, and even Arab woman. Aucks laugh and say how it have a world meeting of woman. Was a funny laugh he had. He would bend forward a little and wheeze, tensing up his chest and thing. He was a real sweet man, always getting the nice woman.

We start to drink Scotch (was a month-end, Aucks get pay and want to make style), and a sweet brown-skin niceness working behind the bar start to watch me like I holding big money or something. Aucks say, *Open a account*, and she say, *No problem.*

But Aucks, I say, *we should have come here first!* Aucks laugh and say how it have fight warm-up and drink warm-up. Tonight we lucky

– we get both. *Ass*. He did have style, though, and so he uses to try and impress me with it. One time – or so Aucks *say* – he tell his father he go leave his car mechanic business if he don't want to expand and start fixing fancy car, too. Aucks tell him he go open up a next place and run him into the ground. The old man study he brains and fix-up fast, yes. Soon Aucks was making three times the money fixing sports car and Benz and thing – don't ask me how he get the mechanics for such a work. He was always saying he had a job line up for me, but it was only when the hard times hit and shake up the whole island that he offer me a job. The job I tell you 'bout.

Anyhow, reggae was shaking the Garden of Eden and woman was looking restless. I swear in them days I uses to be able to see them bristling, sometimes. A young thing brush past me, glittering – like she dressmaker sprinkle a set of diamonds all over this black, tight business she wearing. And earrings. If you see earrings – hanging almost down to she shoulder, in a triangular shape, looking like gold. They was swinging from cheek to neck. Aucks see her and smile. The woman smile back.

And check how the chats uses to go, eh.

Hello, Aucks say.

Hello, she say.

Hello, I say.

The reggae sweet, eh? she say.

The best, Aucks say.

You have a friend? I say.

She smile and say yes, she have a friend who real nice and going university in Washington D.C. and I must ask her to dance. All this time she only eyeing up Aucks like she want to make his child. She had big eyes and a bright smile, pretty as butterfly on a hibiscus flower.

I ask, *Your friend pretty and nice like you?*

She laugh like she shy or something, but her teeth shine bright in the bar light. *You will see,* she say. Just before she walk off she tell we her name is Simonette.

Aucks, Aucks say.

Nello, I say.

Okay, back in a while, she say, and into a crowd of man she gone, and they step aside like she is the Queen of England.

Boy, that *is woman,* Aucks say. *She was design by a architect.* And then he stop, think, look at me and say, *Nello, this place nice, eh? This island is Paradise!*

But in them days I had hear them words so much my head uses to hurt every time somebody say it – whether on the radio, the TV, in a bar – no matter where it was, and I would ask myself if anybody know what really going on in this island. Is the same question the Professor and his friend CC still asking the country in the newspapers. When they find out what it is really going on, what the latest scandal is, then the next question does start, *What we go do, Nello, what we go do?*

We order two more Scotches and lean up on the bar like proper boss. The deejay start to play some nasty calypso and the crowd go wild, like is Carnival already and they was in prison and get pardon or something. If you see people bump and grind each other. A man lift a woman up in the air and try to balance she on his head and the skirt like it suffocate him and they fall down on the ground. The whole place shaking like is earthquake going on. People start to climb up on the bar and dance and scream and shout for all the world to see. The barmen by then, and the owner – everybody except security outside – drunk-drunk, so they don't mind. Madness.

Total *madness:* like people only want to dance their life away. Not just the night, eh. Their whole *fockin'* life.

And to hell with the damn island.

If the professor and CC was there, they would have bawl for we future.

Next thing I hear a squeaky voice behind me. I turn round. Is Simonette. Well, look at luck tonight! She friend even more pretty than she. Her name was Beverly, or so she say, tall and firm with brown short hair. She was wearing a green and black dress, with bow on the shoulder, and it wasn't tight-tight like Simonette own. And Beverly smile did have more style, like she was bring up proper. I feel she must be spend time in England, because she wasn't bold like we islanders and Americans could be. But Aucks didn't like how she smile because he screw up he face as if he smell dead dog on the highway. Aucks had always tell me he didn't like female sophisticate – is trouble they born to make. But from the time I see how Beverly only watching at me – she did have a funny small smile at the corner of her mouth – I say I is a lucky man.

"Nello, I can't find the rum nowhere, man. What you do with it?"

He reach, at last. Mervyn looking too thin these days, but he still moving round all right. He's a tall feller, so the thinness making him more tall.

"Sit down. Rest yourself, Mervyn."

"The night pretty, eh, Nello?"

"You know how long it waiting for you, man?"

Mervyn suck he teeth. And right then I realize I say the wrong thing. Fock. So quick-quick I say, "It waiting for all of we."

Mervyn shake he head little bit from side to side. He's a nice-looking feller, with high cheek bones and a strong jaw like Jack Palance, the American actor who uses to be in plenty Western movies long time. Except Mervyn don't look mean like Palance. He gentle-looking, real black, and slim, as if he is Palance good side.

"Is where you hide the rum, Nello?"

"You check in the cupboard in the bathroom upstairs, on the top shelf?"

Is the onliest place the boys don't really go, because is the bathroom Brother Michael and Sister Maureen does use when they visiting.

"Yeah, but I ain't see nothing."

And then I realise something else 'bout poor Mervyn: since he get sick, like his eyes not working too good. This life not easy, yes.

"Don't worry, I know where it is."

I go upstairs and, sure enough, it there. After he fire two rum, Mervyn sleeping right there in the chair, yes. Good thing the nights not cold.

The rum is the onliest thing what remaining from the paradise this island uses to be.

Aucks end up chatting with Simonette nearly whole night and I end up on the dance floor with Beverly. And she did real like it too, because she was only telling me how she love the moves. And when she ask me 'bout myself, *What do you do?* – she had good English, just like the professor own when he writing proper – I didn't want to dampen the spirit and thing, so I say I in business with Aucks, we making good money and plus extra. Well, she smile like she was real impress with that, but then she say, *You must be careful, the island is a dangerous place these days.* As if I didn't know. But when I tell her the whole world is a dangerous place, she smile bright and pretty again.

Then some more fast tune start to beat up, and Beverly like she not in that, she thirsty, she want a rum and coke. We move over by the bar and is only man watching me and this woman. When woman see their man watching Beverly, they start to give she hard stare. But if you see man watch that woman! I start to feel stupid – like Beverly know all this man, or what? But then I catch myself and realize is only because Beverly so sharp that man watching she so. Then the woman them start to watch me real hard like they wondering how I have a nice woman so. I try to buy Beverly a drink, but like she was one of them independent woman – she buy she own.

Next thing, I see this Selwyn. I first meet him with Aucks. He was plenty trouble even then, so I hide my face, turn to the bartenders, playing cool.

Now, all that time I was only studying how to be alone with Beverly. I was waiting for Aucks to show heself so I could ask him to drop me home with her. And maybe I could put down some good work on she. But things turn out different – *real* different.

At last we come to Selwyn. Selwyn head was *real* bad – like it wasn't just from drinks. He come over to Beverly and me and watch us like he from the Department of Agriculture inspecting beef or something. *Nello!* he say. *How it going?* And Selwyn like he was on some mix of vodka and kerosene, because he make a grab for my balls and say, *How it hanging, Nello? How it hanging?* And he throw back his head and laugh like a real jackass.

I introduce him to Beverly and he roll his eyes and say, *Nello, you going to marry she?*

Selwyn gulp his drink, and like he forget the question.

That night I was only praying Selwyn didn't start to run he mouth 'bout what it was I really doing for Aucks in the car parts business – as if it would have make a blasted bit of difference. So, as best I could, I try to get Selwyn mind off anything 'bout that.

Selwyn, I say, *how your parents? They keeping well?*

Selwyn set up he face like is the wrong thing I bring up.

Look, he say, *don't ask me nothing about my parents. If you see madness when I reach back last night. And I is their only son... yeah.* And he lift he head up a little high, look away like he could shit ice-cream, and gulp he drink.

I ask, *What happen, Selwyn?*

Imagine, they making fuss about the amount of money I spend the last few months. Miami expensive, not so? And he watch Beverly like she does travel everywhere.

Selwyn parents did have money, yes, at least enough to make mine look poor. I always uses to wonder why he didn't get a better education and do something constructive in life.

Now all the time Selwyn talking Beverly giving me glance and thing, as if she wondering how I could have a friend like Selwyn. So I study a plan fast and ask him to take us by my parents' house. My plan was I would borrow the old man car – he wouldn't mind since he sure to be asleep – and take Beverly where she want.

Good, he say. *Let we go. Is sights we going to see.*

And that was my chance to go home with Beverly. Next thing we on the highway in Selwyn sports car doing some mad-ass speed – road only disappearing beneath the car like is a mirage. Beverly was in front holding on to the dashboard for she life.

Could you please slow down, Beverly say.

How you like it, Nello? She could real do numbers, eh!

Look how sweet Mervyn sleeping. Before he start to get weak, I and he uses to sit out here and talk good talks. Now he only dreaming of the next world... What it like, Mervyn? It have rum over there? A man could learn to read easy without hurting his head and get any book he want? And woman, they nice? But for God sake, don't tell me it have nun and priest over there.

A time I ask Sister Maureen what she think Heaven might be like, and she watch me like she feel I 'bout to embrace all the teachings she and Brother Michael carrying on with since I here.

Nello, she say, *it is a place of the utmost bliss and perfection; indescribable, actually; it is where nothing but love eternal thrives. The days have no end of peace and the nights are filled with the most beautiful dreams.*

Sister eyes was real bright when she telling me this, yes, and I did have to confess to myself I did want to put down some work on the woman. It had a time when I uses to wonder what she would look like in regular clothes, as she was a pretty woman, not ugly like most nun is – well, maybe most of them not ugly, eh, pardon me Lord, *if you there*, but they not pretty. But Sister Maureen, I sure she would have make man head swing in Parliament and Garden if she had live a regular life.

But check Mervyn: a dream hold him, he shaking little bit, and the rum bottle clinking against his glass. Let me move the rum bottle before is nightmare the man having and he wake up sudden and lick way the rum, yes.

Man, Selwyn was trouble. Since I meet him, he never take anything serious. Life was just one big joke. A time in Miami, Aucks tell me (this was where he first meet him) Selwyn was telling Louis and Aucks 'bout surfing, surfing the big wave. Louis was a real bright feller, studying engineering on a scholarship – he get big degree with honours – at University of Miami, a place Selwyn uses to call *Unification of Mayhem*. God only know why he call it that, must be something he do there on a visit to Louis.

When Selwyn finish talking 'bout the big wave, Louis start to give him advice, saying how Selwyn must stop wasting his parents' money, start doing something constructive in life. Then Selwyn look at him and say, *But hear nuh, man, Louis! – them waves and them was so high!* And Selwyn stand up on a chair and raise he hands high up in the air like he reaching for the sky.

The man was total slackness. And so he remain.

Louis just laugh, shake he head and say, *Selwyn, is best you just go and live on a beach, yes.*

That night I was only praying Selwyn didn't crash the car, something I wish later had happen in truth. (Well, I didn't wish that for long, yes, for look where I end up. Things might have been much worse.) We pass all the pretty old-time house it have round the Queen's Park Savannah, then we flash by the Hilton Hotel and went up a hill that had a view of the city.

Where we going, Selwyn? I ask.

We going to see the sights, boy!

What do you mean? ask Beverly. *Can you say something else?*
Soon, soon you go see! Selwyn say.

We screech into the car park of a lookout and stop 'bout a foot from the short metal barrier it had by one high-ass cliff overlooking Port of Spain. Some lovers shout at us to behave.

Then Aucks arrive, and I leave Selwyn car with Beverly and get in Aucks own. Selwyn get vex when we get out. He leave first, screeching car tyre again. When I ask Aucks 'bout Simonette, he say she went to the Ladies in Garden of Eden. He wait and wait on her, then he just get out of there because it had too much snake in the place; that is what Aucks uses to say when too much man in Garden. When I ask him how he know where we went, he say Selwyn tell him.

Then it happen. While we going to my house, the police stop us. They search the car. They ask me for my wallet, check my identification. And there I was, standing up bold and stupid, twenty-five years of hardback man with next to no education and only watching the police – two fellers in plain clothes, both with gun, one still with the badge in he hand – and trying to stop myself from cussing. Next thing, like the two police find I acting too relax, too confident – is 'fraid they want me to be. The plumpish one step toward me like I walk into a saloon bar in the Wild West looking for him and Trouble and all Trouble friends. The man start to beat me with the gun-butt in my kidney, asking, *You is somebody? You is somebody? Who the fock you is? You is any focking body?* He beat me 'til I drop on the road, and when he see I not bawlin', he start to kick my face. Man, hear nuh, I see and taste so much of my blood that night it take me a whole month before I could recognize myself in a mirror again. I had was to suck soup through a straw for weeks, because he bust up my mouth terrible with the heel of his boot. Tell me, why people so in this place? But sometimes I think that beat I get was a blessing in disguise, yes, because the next morning when they carry me to the jail, man only watching me like I was somebody in truth for police to beat me so. Nobody interfere with me, like what happen to poor Mervyn, but I know that wasn't lasting long.

The following afternoon, Sister Maureen and Brother Michael arrive with one of them independent senators, and I get out.

They let Aucks go in the morning. They didn't find nothing on him or in the car, so he never get touch really, although I did hear talk they watch him for a while after. But Aucks might have had a couple police in his pocket, so they could have lose any evidence on him – far less get beat like me and then save by priest and nun. Sister Maureen tell me the police say somebody identify me in the Datsun 180B with two of Aucks' "car mechanics" when they steal a Toyota.

I feel was Selwyn, trying to get back at Aucks for something. Must be for some fallout they had between them. Selwyn tip the police and give them some money, I sure. And in this island today, more mad-ass than ever before, it wouldn't surprise me if Aucks and Selwyn try to kill each other already.

See how small man does take the fall for them rich fellers? But I learn a good lesson that night.

And Beverly? I never see or hear 'bout that woman again. She wasn't even in the car with me and Aucks when we went in the station that night.

So that is how I come to be here. Was luck and the goodness of the Organization of Catholics for Reconstructive Action, as I say. But the more I sitting here thinking, is the more I realize the future not looking good. Then again, maybe things will change for the better. I *know* I have to hope so. Is a good thing the Catholics have going here, is something positive, but plenty, plenty more need to be done in this island before it really begin to change. Catholics alone can't save the world.

Mervyn coughing now. Soon he will wake.

I wonder what he dream.

KANAIMA, LATE AFTERNOON

He's alone, driving through sunlight near the Sargasso Sea, the car rising and falling along low hills. Music from the radio lightens his countenance. He's in an ordered, postcard-pretty town. Flowers, triumphant, decorate. He's not thinking of anything in particular.

Now the colours of trees and lawns, and flowers again; now the colours of polite gardens and polite houses; now the colours of moored yachts and docked ships: all are flawlessly lit, seem permanent in this last light.

Now nothing but the openness of sky, the openness of sea: a deep, blue energy. The sea air, windy and voluptuous, buffets the car.

He is in bed. There is not much pain. The drug works well. There is she who watches over him. She smells of earth and flowers, and is gentle like a bright cloud.

The music from the radio continues.

Everything he can see is all right.

The late afternoon light holds; somehow, it still holds.

THE JAGUAR

I would like to be the jaguar of your mountains
And take you to my dark cave.
Open your chest there
And see if you have a heart.
  – old song from Mexico's Yucatan Peninsula

Mid afternoon sunlight filtered through the silk-cotton tree and
onto the jaguar. The cat, a big male, moved in an unbroken
rhythm back and forth along the cage, whiskers almost brushing
the dark iron bars. The end of the jaguar's thick tail looped up a
bit. His jaws were parted for the heat, and his tongue, tip curled
to the roof of his mouth, floated over and under the air he sucked
in and expelled with light gasps.

Roy watched Fiona lean over the waist-high fence, six feet
from the cage, stretching her back and neck toward the animal.
He noted the ridges of her spine through her thin cotton top, and
when the top slid above her jeans, he saw her smooth pale skin,
the tiny footprints of freckles making their way down, he knew,
to run across the right side of her hip, then up again, fading
around her breasts in a splotchy sunset, like a birthmark disintegrating. Just above her hip, reaching for the back of her ribcage,
was the bruise where he had gripped her last night while making
love. It was blue-black and purple tinged, like some fleshy parts
inside the jaguar's mouth.

Fiona stared directly into the jaguar's eyes when it turned at
the corner of its small, square cage. The cat stopped, assessed
Fiona's new position, and returned her gaze with such stillness
and gravitas – eyes unblinking in his steady large head, muscles
tensed as if to throw himself through the cage, the fence, and

onto her – that she straightened, stepped back and took Roy's arm. She tucked some loose strands of light brown hair behind her ear.

"Why'd you suppose he reacted like that?" she asked, her blue eyes startled.

The jaguar resumed strolling, back and forth along the sunlit edge of its cage. A fence sign gave the range of jaguars in the New World, and this one's name: Lollipop. No other information was available.

"Maybe he likes you," Roy said, still brooding over a tense conversation they'd had last night. "Maybe you got too close. Like with De Souza?"

She released his arm. "But he was more beautiful than ever when he did that." Fiona's eyes were bright.

"Really?" Roy frowned. The confines of the jaguar's cage troubled him: it was cruelty, pure and simple. He jingled the car keys in his pants' pocket. "How d'you suppose he'd look if he were a man?" Roy was a little taller than Fiona, but they were on an incline with Fiona upslope, so she was able to lower her head a bit, look Roy straight in the face and ignore him. "Bet you'd want to interview him, too."

"You *are* beginning to whine, dear," she said in the playful voice she'd used earlier to deflate last night's tension. "It's time we visited the monkeys."

Roy followed, feeling as if she were talking to a slightly troubled child. She half-spun to face him, giving her dazzling, genuine smile. He tried to resist, agitated that she could so easily change his mood. Her smile, as natural to her as brooding was to him, made a music in his head – the merry, witty violins of Ireland, her childhood home.

Fiona laughed – an amused appraisal of the situation, perhaps, or maybe she was nervous. He glimpsed the inside of her mouth, her pink tongue, and was almost undone. "Come," she said. "Come along, Jaguar Man." She took his hand, and making deliberate eye contact, said, "Roy, I'd never compromise myself like that. De Souza is a creep. So forget it, all right?"

He wasn't convinced. De Souza was a persuasive man. He wanted Fiona close by and had encouraged her to interview him.

He had warned Roy that perhaps she was not just a journalist for the BBC. Possibly, based on recent scrutiny, Fiona was involved in surveillance work.

An elderly man with a scruffy beard, slim and shirtless, approached, walking purposefully up from the alligator pond. He wore a bright purple scarf, loose khaki shorts and lace-less grey shoes. Halting a few feet from them he fingered his scarf then crossed his long brown arms. His longish hair was matted, with dusty, sun-browned patches that would soon grow into clumps. He smelled of sweat and earth, but it was not unpleasant. His arms were decorated with silver watches strapped tightly from wrists to elbows.

"Good afternoon, Mister Gentleman and Miss Lady. Doctor Edric Traboulay, at your service. This here cat you all was observing so intentionally is best referred to as *Panthera onca*, native to the shores of South and Central America. Very rarely do it harm humans, so please do not be alarmed, Fair One." The man was delighted with them, especially Fiona. He looked proud, licked his upper lip as if relishing his words, and continued. "I taught zoology at the university – long ago." He waved a hand past his head, as though dismissing a whole period of his life. "That was just after the Colonial Administration – the British, you recall?" He looked at Roy.

"Before my time," Roy said, wary of the vagrant. "But of course I remember the Queen's independence visit."

Dr. Traboulay kept his distance, as if sensing that stepping closer would defeat his purpose.

In an impeccable Oxford accent, occasionally interspersed with island dialect, Dr. Traboulay began again. "Ah, the British! Of them I have such *fond* memories! Do you know it was through the good auspices of doctor William Smith – the man who discover five, *five*, of our island hummingbirds. Of the family Trochilidae. Count them." Dr. Traboulay held up his right hand, fingers and thumb splayed, and began to count and name the hummingbirds, lowering each finger as he tapped it. "One, the rufous-breasted hermit, *Glaucis hirsuta*. Two, the black-throated mango, *Anthracothorax nigricollis*. Three, the green hermit, *Phaethornis guy*. Four, the tufted coquette, *Lophornis ornata*. Five, the blue-chinned sapphire, *Chlorestes notatus* – yes!" He gasped, excited by the memory. "Smith was the boss-man of humming-bird, oui. It was because of that decent fellow that I had the good fortune to acquire a scholarship to pursue zoological studies at Oxford University. The *British* – " He stopped and scratched his head, overcome by a troublesome memory. "I was going to tell you about the expedition into the northern range of the island," Dr. Traboulay went on. "But first –" He grimaced and rolled his eyes. "What was it, I wonder…" He looked at the clouds.

Roy and Fiona were both uneasy now. Roy opened his wallet and mumbled, "It's okay." He offered Dr. Traboulay several reddish notes with frolicking scarlet ibises.

"Oh, Sir! You are too kind – but this is entirely unacceptable!" He raised his hand in protest. "First I must tell you my story." He turned away, deep in thought. Roy replaced the money in his wallet.

"Poor man," whispered Fiona. "We should go."

Dr. Traboulay was muttering to himself. He went to the jaguar cage and addressed the cat in Latin. "Pulvis et umbra sumus," he said. The jaguar, still pacing, watched expectantly. The vagrant seemed lost in another world.

Fiona and Roy eased away.

"Have you seen him before?" Fiona asked Roy.

"Not that I remember. But there're a few like him around. He probably moved up from South recently. I doubt he's been in this condition very long. A few years ago a man used to ride around the northwest on a bicycle in a suit of silver foil. You had to wear sunglasses just to look at him. Now he's gone. Perhaps he's elsewhere on the island. Or perhaps they go in and out of these phases."

As Roy and Fiona wandered beneath the huge branches of the silk-cotton tree, they passed a man hosing an agouti cage. When he saw Fiona, he wagged the hose in front him stupidly, calling, "Sweetness. Come by me, nuh."

"Oh fuck," Fiona said, looking away.

Roy, hunching his shoulders and then releasing them in exasperation said, "Good afternoon, sir."

The man ignored him. They walked by.

"When it comes to islands, I think I'm starting to prefer England, Ireland. Even in winter. It's not just crime in general, and all the guns most people seem to have, but what men do to women here that's truly frightening. At the Consulate I saw last year's rape reports. You wouldn't believe –"

"But you said you loved it here, you said –"

She held his arm. "I do, you know, but… maybe it helps with leaving. Come with me." Fiona had asked this before.

Roy lifted his free arm and let it fall helplessly. He tilted his head and saw the sky in gaps through the silk-cotton tree, blue distances, clouds drifting. "A whole island, a whole country," he said, "its problems unassailable. I couldn't listen to poor Dr. Traboulay's story. Sounds like the British treated him better than we did."

Fiona sighed, released his arm. "I imagine with independence, people began hating him for admiring the British."

"No doubt. One of the things my father taught me was to see beyond the way anyone sounded or looked. And for a long time I was able to go anywhere on this island. I looked at people a certain way and they returned it – an unassuming manner. That was the secret. Then he told me it wouldn't last. He was right. Thank God he didn't live to see how we've wrecked things."

"Why 'we'"?

"I never did anything to stop it. I never spoke to people like my father did. Like many others, I suppose, I thought things would work out, that things would be set right. They weren't. There was so much to do, and we never realised." He paused. "Or maybe we knew what had to be done, but just didn't get around to it, for reasons I don't even want to consider now."

"Is that why you won't leave?" Again she waited for an answer. They walked past cages with sleeping macaws, their long blue red and yellow tails cast down, their heads and bodies hidden in the shadowed cool of their perches. He thought of the jaguar's confined pacing, of the vagrant observing the beast with the devotion of the zoologist he had once been. As Roy passed the last cage, a macaw looked at him out of a wrinkled sleepy eye, then stretched and flapped its wings, moving nowhere. Had the bird been a few hundred miles southeast, say in Guyana, a natural habitat, it would soon be gliding for miles along a river before roosting high in the forest canopy. And below, on the forest floor, moving through sun-dappled vegetation would be the jaguar impatient for a night of no moon.

Roy shrugged. "Maybe, in a way, I've already left." Once again, involuntarily, he thought of De Souza.

"Stop," Fiona said. "Not now, with so few days left."

"What does it matter?" he said. "We've had our time, our chance."

"Oh... don't."

"I'm afraid I don't have your restraint, my dear."

Her eyes glistened, but her voice was calm. "Please stop." Taking his arm, she ran her long fingers along its inside. Goose bumps raced the length of his arm, swept up onto his shoulder, tingled his neck, and ended below his left ear. It was like being caressed from beneath the skin, as though his blood were tickling him. Yet he resented this pleasure, resented even her voice sometimes. As their last days burned themselves out, thoughts of facing the island's confines alone spurred him to resist her. And he resented that, as did she. Their lovemaking had become infrequent, but more passionate. They gripped and bit each other, hard. Orgasms were dramas of minor brutalities.

"It's all right," he said, circling an arm around her waist. They stopped and he held her close. "There's still time." Her head was bowed, hair falling on his shoulder and chest. She was sniffling, wiping her eyes. "I can't stand it when you cry, Fiona. Please." He kissed her shoulder. The soft, thin cotton of her blouse met his lips. It tasted of the sea, the hidden beach where they had swum nude yesterday then sipped cold white wine in the shade of an almond tree. As the blue of the ocean deepened, and the sand became the colour of old lions, they'd left, the green mountains darkening in the last light. In the air, in the sky, there was a sweet sadness, the old story of islands: people you loved, or felt you could love, went away. Matters of the heart were interrupted.

"Yes," she lifted her head. "There's still time, isn't there, Roy?" She searched his eyes, but he turned away.

Taking her hand, he squinted at the sky and led her to the green waterfowl pond. Tall clusters of bamboo, many of their leaves burnt orange-brown, arched over their heads, rustling in a late afternoon breeze. The golden sunlight flickered down. He remembered the colours of the jaguar and its small cage. The cat thrived on movement – swimming hundreds of yards, fishing in streams, climbing trees after monkeys, roaming savannahs, mountains.

"You can't come away with me anywhere, can you Roy?"

They crossed a grey wooden bridge, a structure he'd known since he was a child, and two swans, one black, one white, glided from beneath, silent as sunlight. "Look at them," Fiona murmured. "They have no room to run, to become airborne." She stared at Roy.

Their long, elegant necks, their grace, even here, captivated him.

Fiona had to say goodbye to people, attend dinners, drop off videos, pack and arrange shipping. Still, she and Roy spent a few afternoons on the coast, avoiding discussion about her inevitable departure. But the sea's distances, its green coast extending for miles into towering veils of haze, drew it from them. They bickered, attempting to gauge each other's feelings. Then late at night, after one or two bottles of wine, they made their love.

Roy had hoped the zoo would be a distraction as well as settle their debate about the jaguar's range. Fiona thought the early colonists had killed them off, but Roy was uncertain. Years ago the zoo manager told him that jaguars had never inhabited Trinidad. Yet the island was only a few miles from South America, and jaguars were excellent swimmers. Roy's father used to tell a story of a jaguar crossing near the mouth of Guyana's Demerara River, a distance of over two miles. And surely jaguars had roamed in pre-Columbian times before the land connection to South America sank. Roy thought, by now, more information would be available. The current zoo manager, a young, worried-looking East Indian in sneakers, khaki trousers and a blue open-necked shirt, didn't know.

"Man, like you is the first person I ever hear ask such a question, yes. You all from foreign?" Roy was about to answer when the manager turned to Fiona, and no response was required. Fiona winked at Roy as the manager spoke freely. "I think

121

it might have had one or two that was here. I hear a story that one drift across from Venezuela on a clump of trees, but some fellers in South shoot it fast. If that was happening regular before Columbus reach, maybe the Carib Indians kill them out. And what they didn't kill, the Spanish would have kill, while killing the Caribs. As for jaguar bones, maybe no one ever really look." He laughed regretfully. "It had all kind of madness in this place, yes. People who didn't want to kill people they was living with here wanted to make money off them. Was that come first. And with all the crime we having these days, like it still going on."

"But what about the ocelots?" Fiona asked brightly "There are still some on the island, and they grow to near half the size of an adult jaguar, I think."

"Is true, yes – it have ocelot too all about in Venezuela, Guyana and Central America." The zoo manager wondered about it, nodding.

Roy was going to thank the manager when someone yelled, "Boss! The bush doc reach *again*!"

"Oh God, man. Not Daniel in the Den of Lions again." The manager, looking back at Roy and Fiona, started in the direction of the big cats. A dark, barebacked figure was hastening away, silver glinting along his brown arms.

"Excuse," the manager said. "Poor old fellah, his mind not too good. Last week he enter the lion den and start telling them about Africa. Good thing we had feed them already." The manager tapped his head, smiled at Fiona, and jogged off, shirt collar rising around his ears like little wings, his buttocks undulating in their tight trousers.

Still earlier that afternoon, in hills overlooking the western coast, Roy headed from his mother's secluded home to Fiona's apartment. He considered his mother: two years into widowhood, abandoned by her husband's friends, ostracized by the island women who guarded their too-contented husbands with a furtive wickedness, she had emigrated to Miami where two of her sisters lived. She had sold half of her husband's business interests and signed the rest over to Roy with the stipulation he consult her before selling. Roy wanted to sell for a fair price to Norman De

Souza, Minister of National Security, but the Minister preferred the current arrangement he had with Roy, whose direct participation had been deemed "necessary for continued success". It was a matter of security, he had said, until Roy would agree to sell at a significantly lower price. *They are the ones you "say no" to,* Roy's father had written in his diary which Roy discovered after De Souza had intimidated him into laundering money through his businesses. *Learn to see. Watch closely. Then learn to "play no", not say it. Or better, misunderstand them. Act the fool. It's your only chance.*

Roy mulled over Fiona's imminent departure, steeling himself for its inevitability, and pondered why she had come to the island. Six months earlier the BBC had sent her to Trinidad to research a documentary on the impact of drug trafficking on the island's economy. She liaised with the British Consulate where she met Roy at a symposium on money laundering. De Souza had introduced them. Later, when De Souza realised he couldn't sleep with Fiona, he became uneasy with her questions. He couldn't understand her lack of fear. *Don't you read the newspapers, darling? One doesn't pry into the drug trade. Do you know where you are? This isn't jolly old England, you know. And even there, now...*

But at the symposium, an elegant sense of class and decorum had prevailed, an awareness by most everyone of everyone's importance, and, especially, of one's own importance. New information was presented: 30-40% of the island's dollar was drug based; some five to ten metric tons of cocaine were shipped through each month, with 15-25% distributed on the island; drug shipment interdiction hadn't increased in five years; money laundering was now so lucrative that it had become impossible to arrest anyone notable; major crime connected with the drug trade, prostitution and arms-trafficking, had risen significantly in the last five years. One suggested solution was to have secure hotlines for reporting suspicious activity. At this, Roy noticed some men in the audience smile.

Roy had watched De Souza – two rows ahead in a pale grey Armani suit, jowls appropriately puffed over his collar, gold signet ring glinting – scribbling away in a notebook. His profile registered the concern of the powerful under the public gaze. A national television report following the symposium featured ten seconds of footage of politicians, businessmen, and De Souza and Fiona shaking hands. Fiona was to "produce a tourism documentary with a keen interest in safety".

At the reception Fiona meandered toward Roy and De Souza, as they ate curried shrimp pierced with toothpicks and wrapped in pink hibiscus petals. "Have you met Miss Hamilton, Roy?" De Souza had asked softly and then grinned, his mouth full.

"Not yet," Roy said, wanting to be far away from everyone there.

"She's with the BBC." He chuckled. "I'm going to be showing her around, of course. Ah, Miss Hamilton."

Roy turned. She was tall and wore green slacks and a black, long-sleeved blouse, low-cut. Her eyebrows were long, shapely. Eye contact was instant. Her hand reached toward him so he had to look at her eyes immediately. She stared with intense, brief passion, like someone who'd fleetingly glimpsed horror – the expression concentrated in her grey-blue eyes, moist and unblinking. She might be on cocaine, Roy mused. Then with easy poise she glanced at De Souza, who had been looking at her prominent and flushed breasts. "Delighted to meet you," Fiona said to Roy. The tight grip of her handshake made him curious.

"And you," Roy managed to say.

"The Minister has told me all about you." Fiona lifted a glass of wine from a silver tray as an indifferent waiter strolled by. De Souza was not liked.

"And have I been good?" Roy asked, playing along.

"That depends," De Souza said, "on your plans." The Minister winked at Fiona, his eyes unable to convey their boyish charm so used-up of late.

"And what are your plans?" Fiona asked Roy.

Roy shrugged, trying to smile like a good-natured fool. "Up to my partner here. Is there anything we can help you with?"

"Matters of safety," Fiona said.

The Minister was scanning the room. "I can't seem to get a drink," he complained. He snapped his fingers at a waiter who seemed to be deliberately avoiding him.

Roy gave her a week. She called after four days.

Roy drove under towering roadside trees, dipped below the view of distant sea, and began to smell the village at the foot of the hills, wood smoke and the sweet-stink of garbage. A natural stream ran alongside the road. A small reservoir that had once been the water source for the village lower down and the wealthy houses in the hills was now abandoned. The village depended on the stream which began high in the mountains, in mist-cool, fragrant forests he'd seen as a boy. An evergreen, almost pre-Columbian world existed there, though today it was higher in the mountains and further away. Fantastic flowers, variously spurred, lobed and pouched, abounded; some were epiphytes, bulging with purple, red and blue. As a teenager he'd been reminded of their textures and colours when he first saw between the legs of a woman. In a somewhat intoxicated trancelike state in the dimly lit room, he'd stroked her and whispered, "Botany."

"What?" She'd lifted her dark, beautiful head.

So he'd breathed her name. "Annalee."

"Up here, silly," she'd replied.

The land, rising steeply on either side of the road, held bush and trees, but these trees were smaller than the old-forest ones Roy had passed higher up. Sections of the sloping earth were planted with vegetables and fruit trees. Shacks rested on stones and bricks. Overhead the treetops met so the entire area was shaded, and the stream, wider here with occasional glints, trickled and swished. Roy crossed a narrow bridge. Below, dark-skinned young women sitting on rocks were washing clothes. Others, scantily clad in bras and panties, were bathing. Two of the bathers waved and smiled. Shaking themselves, they asked if he wanted them.

After the bridge, after the stream, the women and cool shadows, the road entered hard sunlight. The land opened and dwellings became concrete, but the sense of hardship remained. Few houses were painted. Around a bend boys ran and shouted at him, moving their cricket game in the road just enough for him to pass. One spat on the windshield as Roy slowed.

"Gone!" another yelled.

Then Roy saw Freddie moving smoothly and quickly, tall, too slim, dread-locked Freddie, resident drug dealer, called Red Boy when he was a child, and now a member of an armed gang with political connections. As children he and Roy had hunted in the green mountains. Freddie waved for Roy to stop and ordered the boys back. "Them don't know, eh," Freddie nodded. "Times change."

"Freddie." They bumped fists.

"Pass some water on the windshield, Boss."

Roy hesitated then sprayed the windshield. Water and light thickened on the glass, and briefly, the world went out of focus. Freddie pulled a rag from his pocket, saying, "Leave the wipers. Lemme show them little bitches we is friends." Roy felt foolish watching his childhood friend, who'd taught him to make slingshots, wipe the glass in front of him. He glanced at the boys. They stood apart, silent, mystified and respectful. Freddie wrung the rag and said, "Gervase."

"Freddie?"

"Come." Freddie tucked the rag back into his trousers, leaving most of it exposed to dry. A boy of maybe twelve stepped forward, trembling. "*Come*, I say!"

Gervase, head lowered, came closer.

Roy shifted and said, "Freddie –"

"Chill, breds," Freddie replied, raising a palm. Then to Gervase, "Watch Mr. Gonzales' son. You hear your mammy talk 'bout Mr. Gonzales, right?" Years ago Roy's father had given Freddie's parents financial assistance.

Gervase nodded.

"You hear Moses talk 'bout him, right?"

Gervase nodded again.

"And you hear I talk 'bout him too, not so?"

The boy nodded once more.

"This Roy, Mr. Gonzales' son. Watch him." Gervase raised his head and looked at Roy.

Roy acknowledged the boy with a half smile.

"Gone," Freddie said. Gervase turned but was unable to miss the slap from Freddie's heavy hand. It caught the back of his head just beneath his right ear. He staggered, dropped to his knees, then rose and ran up the road.

Freddie reached for Roy's hand on the steering wheel and held it between his palms. He bent to Roy. "Praise," Freddie said. "Praise. I remember your father, I remember you."

"Okay," Roy said, wanting to go.

Freddie said, "How the lady? De Souza talk with you lately?"

Roy told him Fiona was fine, and that he hadn't spoken with De Souza. Should he have?

"Let you know later, breds." Roy thanked him and drove off.

Twenty-five minutes later, in her apartment in a sealed-off compound whose entrance was guarded, Fiona greeted Roy. He had been thinking about his meeting with Freddie and his discussion with Fiona the night before about De Souza.

Fiona stared. "Are you all right?" Roy's face was drawn. His arms rose for her and they embraced. "Roy," she whispered. "Roy, talk to me."

He did, but not about his father, Freddie or De Souza. Then, after a cold drink, they went to the zoo.

It was four-thirty. They were sipping beer at a table outside the tuck shop, half-hoping the zoo manager would return so they could learn more about Dr. Traboulay. Lovers had carved devotions into the old wooden tabletop. Fiona's elegant middle finger circled the lip of her beer bottle carelessly, then slid to the label loosened with condensation.

Roy watched her intently. "Did you interview De Souza?"

"I did." Her eyes were mischievous, still focused on the bottle.

"I knew it." Roy sat back, crestfallen. "Doesn't sound like a good move to me, especially as he wants to get you into bed."

Fiona's expression changed. "At one point the phone rang, and he had to step out. From the look on his face I knew there was no surveillance in the room. Also, he couldn't return in less than two minutes. And of course, there were the steps, creaky old wooden ones... dear things."

"You *went* to his *house*?"

"Of course, darling."

Roy shook his head and huffed. "Who did you have call?"

She shrugged her shoulders, winked.

"He must really regret the day he met you."

"Do you?" Fiona lifted her face.

But Roy asked, "What did you find?"

She gave him her dazzling smile, exactly like the one at the jaguar's cage earlier, and tapped her temple. "When he returned, he was completely flustered. We chatted a bit; I asked a few more questions, then I got up to leave. He walked me to the door." Fiona drank the last of her beer. "He tried to kiss me."

Roy paled. He glanced around and stood. "Let's get out of here. All these cages make me sick."

"Oh?" Fiona put her bottle down and rose. "Oh," she said demurely. She took his arm. "Kiss me."

Roy didn't. He was unsure where she was going with this.

Fiona said seriously, "He actually *did* try to kiss me."

Roy stepped away. "Stop it." But his words lacked conviction. Something else bothered him. "Did you go through his desk?" He faced away from her, staring into the confines of the tuck shop.

"He grabbed my tits, shoved his hand between my legs, and tried to drool on my mouth. I kicked him where he deserved."

Roy tried to stay calm. "Oh, so you didn't go through his desk?"

"Can't you ask something else?"

"We should go." He took her arm and began striding to the exit.

"Okay. I'm sorry I didn't tell you before. I was just doing my job. Didn't think you'd be so interested."

He jerked her to a halt. "And *what* do I have to do to show I'm interested, *really* interested, Fiona, tell me."

"Are you jealous?"

Roy didn't reply. A heavy-set man came past. He wore hiking boots, new jeans and belt, his brand name jersey a dark navy blue. His right hand worked a toothpick protruding from his mouth; the left was half-inserted into a front pocket. He nodded, one stranger to another on a pleasant afternoon. "All right."

"Okay," Roy replied.

Fiona glanced at the man as Roy pulled her along, increasing his pace and not looking back. They passed the waterfowl pond. At the exit, as they hurried through the turnstile, Fiona whispered to Roy, asking if he'd brought his gun. Roy ignored her. He hit his knee on one of the lower bars and cursed. As they got in the car, under the massive spreading branches of a samaan, Fiona was visibly nervous, looking back at the exit. Roy drove, thinking of somewhere peaceful close by.

"Roy, what's wrong? Are we being paranoid?"

"Tell me."

She was silent.

The car, at the edge of a circular unmarked car park, ticked with heat from the winding ascent. Roy and Fiona leaned against a low rock wall. They were alone. A burnt-out building, roofless, its peeling concrete pillars intertwined with vines, stood to their left and a little lower down. It had once been, from World War II to the late 1960s, a fashionable restaurant to visit on afternoons and evenings. As a child Roy had sat in the large, open-top verandah of the restaurant with his mother. The waiters had worn black trousers and white, long-sleeved shirts with bowties. Roy had asked for a coke, sat sipping it through a straw while his mother, in golden sunlight, spoke about the black and white photographs of famous people over the bar. The gulf, then, had been bluer.

He could see several valleys of the northern range descending to the gulf. Hovels, set on the valleys' slopes, faded in and out of the hazy air. The scent of kerosene fires, garbage and dust, drifted up the hillsides. Subdued reggae and Baptist bells mingled, made a steady throb, as of a distant party, one he'd been hearing since childhood. It was a part of the background hum of the city. It was as though, once begun at the foot of the hills, the party could never cease, must overwhelm the hills and valleys, beating on and on, its hovels eating into the earth of the island.

Before them the land sloped down to the city far below, and to the harbour, where the hulks of several shipwrecks lay side up. Long feathery grass, green and brown-tinted and like young sugarcane in texture, rippled in a light breeze, moving in great spreading greens down the hillside, dry-brown tints reflecting gold, a child's version of a sea. They both watched it. Some of the last mountains of the northern range, the highest on the island, rose dark and silent behind them, the beginning of another world.

"Are you involved with De Souza?" Fiona asked quietly.

"I'm acquainted with him. We see each other at meetings, conferences, like the one where we met. You know that."

"That's not what I'm asking, and you know it."

Roy shrugged. "The rumours are there. This place is loaded with them. It's a way of life here. How can people not make assumptions? It's how the island amuses itself, Fiona." Roy hesitated. "There's no evidence on De Souza. You couldn't have seen anything in his house. And even if you had, you wouldn't have taken it."

"Damn right I took nothing. But I saw something."

He waited.

"An address book with names of members of the judiciary, the business elite – your father among them – and contacts in Antigua, Curacao, St. Maarten. There were also Russian names, fax numbers, phone numbers – many crossed out, some not – and odd names, like nick names or codes."

Roy scratched the side of his neck, gripped the skin between his thumb and forefinger, and pinched. "So De Souza, who once did business with my father, and does on occasion with me, De Souza, who's presently buying paint for condos he's sprucing up in South – and don't ask me where he got the money – De Souza, who was at the signing of the drug treaty with the Americans three years ago, this De Souza you think is a criminal? And as for the Russians, they're everywhere these days. Look at what they've been through. I mean, so what if he has those contacts. He should. He's in government and he's a businessman."

She was quiet. Then she asked, "Roy, do you love me?"

A few vultures, their wings fixed like black machetes, glided southward over the ruined restaurant. For the last five hundred years, Roy thought, this image was the most consistent for the Caribbean, South America and Central America.

The tall grass rustled near Fiona. She shrank back against Roy. Out of the bush, separating it with a walking stick, and head held high, walked Dr. Edric Traboulay, his wristwatches reflecting the last of the afternoon sunlight.

"Ah! We meet again! I am presently experiencing a period of reasonable clarity," he announced. "Those hummingbirds I mentioned earlier, *these* were the mountains Dr. William Smith and I climbed in search of them, but more to the east." He waved the stick in the general direction. "Funny, but I still can't recall the story I wanted to tell you at the zoo. My mind, these days, makes its own random selections. My will is beside the point! Anyway, during the dry seasons of the 1950s we did not experience such arid conditions as occur today after every Christmas season. Hence we were able to travel comfortably, as there were few fires during that time." He stood the stick in front of him, resting his hands on its gnarled end, his watches glinting in the sunlight like the arm-sheaths of a knight. Roy wondered if the watches worked. Dr. Traboulay looked up at the mountains, his eyes soft, as if lost in some fond memory. Thin cuts from the tall grass crisscrossed his upper arms and ribs. Sweat dripped from his brow.

Fiona said, "You're back, sir." She glanced at Roy, appearing unsure of everything around her.

"Please, Miss Lady and Mr. Gentleman, I mean no harm. I don't often get to talk to such nice people. How, may I ask, did Lollipop seem?"

Roy said, "Who?"

"Oh! Forgive me. The jaguar, his name is Lollipop – at least that's what *some* people think. Someone removed my sign last month. I made another then, but the new manager refused to put it up. He said it did not cater to the public's tastes. What, I ask, is wrong with a little poetry by Blake?"

"'Tyger tyger, burning bright'?" Fiona asked, relaxing.

Dr. Traboulay's eyes lit up. "Precisely, my dear! Just because Blake was writing about the Indian tiger does not mean the poem cannot be applied to Lollipop, a name I strongly recommend they change. But, alas, the manager will not hear of it. I haven't given up, though. Imagine calling a jaguar Lollipop! You might as well name him Popsicle, or Kit Kat, names not worthy of the status of the jaguar. Surely this is obvious." Dr. Traboulay, chin up, awaited response.

Fiona said, "I agree."

"It's a very beautiful animal," Roy added.

"Exactly. You both are educated," Dr. Traboulay continued, "unlike these foolish politicians, little boys they are. I'd send them back to school, if I could. Nothing but a bureaucratic herd determined to master mediocrity – and *worse*."

"And I'd help you," Roy said, thinking of De Souza while edging to the passenger side of the car where Fiona had left the window down. "Perhaps you can tell us another story," he suggested. Roy's phone and a revolver were in the locked glove compartment. He slipped his hand in his pocket, and when Dr. Traboulay turned to look at the ruined restaurant, quickly removed the keys and unlocked the glove compartment. He stayed leaning on the car door, uncertain of Dr. Traboulay's intentions.

"Everywhere I go these days, I recall another story, though details, some quite significant, often elude me," Dr. Traboulay said. "My walk here was filled with memories, many I'd not recalled for ages. Chapters of my life sailed through my mind, around every corner, under every tree… They came to me out of the blue, literally." He laughed. "I am rather partial to the odd cliché, now and then, if you'll excuse me." He walked toward the ruined restaurant. "For instance, this relic. I mean –" halting he broke off, became flustered, mumbled to himself in Latin, then reverted to the local dialect. "Jew man get he place burn down. Investigation say is arson. Police Commissioner tell the Jew man to leave. *Just so*. And the insurance get seize." Now he said, continuing to walk, "The ways of the business community on this island have never ceased to amaze me."

Watching Dr. Traboulay's back, Roy got the revolver and phone from the glove compartment. He dropped the phone on the seat and pocketed the gun, then followed him. Fiona indicated the gun. "Just to be safe," he whispered.

She slipped an arm around Roy's as they joined Dr. Traboulay who raised his stick at the ruins. "Allow me to tell you something about this restaurant. It was at the height of its popularity in 1960 shortly before Marlene Dietrich came out with, 'Where Have All the Flowers Gone?' I remember a beautiful woman showing up here with a little boy, a few years after that. She looked like Ava Gardner. I think it might have been you and your mother. Dr. Traboulay pointed a silver-glinting arm at Roy. "She resembled you. A dark and brooding look."

Roy nodded, managing to smile. "Possible."

"That is so. And memories are everywhere you turn. Too many for me now, though." Dr. Traboulay sighed, began again. "I was a waiter, had started working here in the mid-1950s when I met Dr. William Smith at the bar one afternoon. Quite by chance we spoke about hummingbirds, about the fauna and flora of the island. He hired me as his assistant the following week. The restaurant gained some notoriety when Ernest Hemingway visited one evening. He was on his way back from Peru. Very decent to me he was! He asked many questions about the island, its natural history. He was returning to Cuba, and when I asked if he was sympathetic to Fidel Castro, he smiled and said yes, it was time. Sure enough, four years later – confusions within confusions." Dr. Traboulay waved a hand past his head. "There was a picture of Ernest and his wife over the bar. I have never met such a free spirit. There was something remarkably human, *good* about him and, as I learned after his death, something mean and cruel. People were so eager to judge his character. His work suffered as a result. Is nothing sacred? Sad the way he died. But they say there's nothing quicker than a gunshot to the head. Is that not correct?" His tone was sombre. He looked at Roy.

An early evening cool encircled them, a wind fresh with earth and sea, flowing down from the green mountains. The tall grass swayed. The haze of grey-white light over the gulf was gone. The horizon of sea and sunset was shades of grey, pale blue and gold, with hints of lavender. Far to the south, pulsing out of the almost purple late-afternoon land, orange flames from the oil refinery became visible; they seemed, in the haze still suspended above the land, to be tongues lapping through from another dimension, like devils testing a new frontier. All was quiet. The Baptist bells had subsided as the dusk deepened. The sounds of dogs were softer, more intermittent. The scent of wood smoke and kerosene was gone, breezed away. The certainty of night came upon them. Roy sensed something of what the conquistadors must have felt during their first nights on the island: the absolute promise of an infinity of tomorrows, to which no one would belong, of course, but the conquistadors would not have thought that; they had believed themselves righteous men, engaged in an ordained enterprise, one commanded by Her Catholic Majesty, and, therefore, approved by God. All the world's tomorrows belonged to them.

"Are either of you partial to oysters?" Dr. Traboulay was regarding the ruins sadly, lost in his own thoughts. Fiona, trying to enjoy the view, had shifted closer to Roy.

Roy said, "I imagine most people are."

Dr. Traboulay, moving his head slowly from side to side, said, "They tasted better in the days of the restaurant, more like a clean sea." He held up his hand, curling the fingertips to caress his palm. "In the days of this restaurant, we had such oysters. They had more life then. The salt was better."

"Do you still eat them?" Fiona asked. "There must be somewhere the sea is still okay."

"Yes, but… but… it is not the same…" He tapped the side of his head. "It is horrible, sometimes, to *know* things. I learned too much. The British were great collectors of knowledge. And they shared it with me. But then came independence, and – and – it was good. Yes, it was. But only for a while, only for a while. The new rulers came to hate everything, including the knowledge on which my profession is built. To them it was colonial knowledge, you see. They hated it all, especially with the oil boom. There was nothing we could not buy. They set me up at the university; they ruined my life. I was a flaneur in my profession, in the strict traditional French sense. Then, almost overnight, the nation – if that is the right word for a place like this – became a flaneur in the present English sense. And so we remain, lapsing, a ghetto country, adrift and in awe of Almighty America when it pleases us. And so…" he waved at distant hovels in the valley, at the sea changing into a last shade of blue; and the orange tongues of flame, brighter now, in the far south of the island. "We remain slaves, occasionally bringing a glimmer of amusement even to the most liberal eye."

Dr. Traboulay shuddered and slapped his matted head repeatedly as if trying to shake out something inside. Again he reverted to local dialect. "It have too much thing inside this head. Mankind is a sinful beast, yes." He moved toward the bushes from which he had emerged earlier.

Roy watched, hands in pockets. "Excuse me," Dr. Traboulay

said, "I must visit my aunt. I shall return shortly." He nodded and disappeared into the tall grass.

"We should be going soon, I guess," Roy said, relieved.

"It's odd, but I think I'd feel better about that poor man, about the world, if I knew he was really angry about something. It's so sad to be damaged like that."

"Maybe he was angry. A long time ago." Roy, hands still in his pockets, gazed at the distant gulf. He thought Fiona would question him, but she didn't.

Dr. Traboulay reappeared. He went to the rock wall, hoisted himself up and sat. Then he bowed his head, clasped his hands and began to mumble.

"He's praying," Fiona said. She blinked several times then wiped her eyes.

The phone chimed. Roy went to the car and answered, leaning against the car door, watching Fiona to his left in front of the ruins and Dr. Traboulay some ninety feet ahead on the wall. Freddie's voice was crisp, more alive than when he'd seen him.

"Boss," Freddie said. "Souza call. He head hot. Like jumbie hold him."

Roy swallowed. "I'm listening."

"Miss Fiona do something. He in a state."

"A little misunderstanding. Nothing to worry about. I'll see about it."

"Better hear this first," Freddie said, his voice rising. "Souza say you *don't want to know* what Miss Fiona really wrap up with."

Roy tried to think. "Tell him not to be concerned. I know what he's worried about, and I've checked it out. All harmless."

Fiona began walking over to Dr. Traboulay. A strand of her hair lifted by the wind caught the last light then curved around her face, across the tip of her nose. She stopped near the doctor, leaned against the wall and spoke. Roy could not hear her.

"Well, Boss," Freddie said, "that is you and he business."

A pause.

"You know I will help you how I could," Freddie continued. "But is only so far I could go, you understand. Me and the fellahs watching out for you, but Souza like he watching everybody these days. Best thing to do now is get the lady out fast."

Roy coughed, thinking.

"Boss?"

"You have anything on a Dr. Traboulay? Vagrant fellah, educated, maybe mad?"

"I hear about him. They call him Watchman, for all them watch on his hand. Know the time all round the world. He does be all about, but he in North a year now. He know plenty thing, like history nuh, and about bird and animal. It had a fellah like that in the Bahamas fifteen years ago. He cause plenty trouble. Fockin' man was suppose to be blind, yes, but he was workin' for the DEA. Anyhow, Souza calling you just now, eh."

"Right. Thanks."

Freddie clicked off. Roy walked around the car twice, counting to himself. Fiona and Dr. Traboulay hadn't stopped talking. The phone rang again. He counted to five before answering.

"How are we, Roy?" De Souza's smooth voice filled his ear.

"There's a problem?"

"In our business, there's no such thing, Roy, only solutions. Kind of unfortunate, but there you are."

Silence.

"How was the zoo?" De Souza asked.

"Needs maintenance, as usual. It's one problem that'll never be solved, but it works fine, doesn't attract much attention. Which is the way I thought we liked things."

"Do you recall, Roy, the time I took you to meet God in Miami? Recall, if you can, the movie theatre for the special preview, the scent of the people, especially the women, Roy. You said – and I've never forgotten this – that if Heaven is a place, this is how it would smell. To me it was the scent of – how shall I put it? – utmost security. Power. Of never having to worry about anything. Rolex watches glinted in the dim light. The women were 'Heaven scent'. I laughed when you said that. You've always had a way with words, Roy, words and women. It's a talent you should use a little more wisely, especially when it comes to Fiona."

He sensed De Souza thinking: a faint sigh combined with some static, which was unusual for De Souza's connections.

"So how is He?" Roy asked. "How is God?"

"He still resides in Miami, knows your mother socially. It's not a very warm acquaintance, despite her devotion to the church. It's an appropriate one, however, unlike yours with Fiona."

"Exactly what's on your mind, De Souza?"

"There're a few matters I'm concerned about."

"I assure you there is nothing to worry about. Fiona told me everything. It's nothing but schoolgirl drama." Roy winced. "She still has bit of a crush on you."

Fiona and Dr. Traboulay were now silhouettes against the dark blue light, talking to one another. The doctor had straightened from his hunched position and now faced Fiona who stood attentively a few feet away, arms folded.

"Good. Very good, Roy. Now tell me about our resident zoologist. Or is it anthropologist?"

"Harmless," Roy said. "For Christ's sake, you're really tense. Get a massage or something."

"I'm leaving the matter entirely in your hands, Roy. I'm leaving for Miami tomorrow. I'm taking the good word to Him. I have faith in you. As does He." De Souza coughed. "Roy?"

"Here."

"I did warn you about our mutual lady friend."

"Yes. Say hello to my mother."

De Souza clicked off.

Roy tossed the phone onto the car seat and began walking toward Fiona and Dr. Traboulay.

Dr. Traboulay was saying, "It was Conrad, my dear, who said, 'All ambitions are lawful except those which climb upwards on the miseries or credulities of mankind.' To that we must add the animal kingdom and the remaining beauty of this island. If we lose them, we lose ourselves." The doctor's words trailed into the evening air.

It was cool. The mountains were dark, austere.

Roy, do you love me? He was trying to think.

The jaguar stopped pacing. The zoo's nocturnal captives were restless in the darkness. He sensed their movements, confined as his own, and stood tall on his hind legs, front paws against the cage, observing. The moon had not yet risen. A scent of salt lingered on the sign the man had attached to the upper part of his cage. No one had been around then, and the man – who spoke Latin, sounds similar to those that accompanied the first real intrusion into the jaguar's environment over five hundred years ago, but that afternoon a gentle music – had given him salt, which the jaguar licked from his palm. Then the man attached a black wooden sign onto the jaguar's cage, weaving a strong cotton string, tied to nails in the sign, around the bars. Now the jaguar, standing seven feet tall, was looking through the bars, his heavy head and jaws by the sign. Occasionally, smelling a faint scent of salt, the jaguar licked the sign, his eyes half-closing, affectionate almost.

The moon rose.

In careful white script, the sign read:

For centuries the jaguar has been associated with human fears and desires. In Mesoamerica, around 1200 B.C., Olmec art was dominated by human-jaguar forms resembling werewolves. After the Mayan conquest, images of the jaguar, *balam*, thought to be the manifestation of the night sun under the earth, guarded tombs, temples, and thrones. The Aztec culture's warrior elite was called the Jaguar Knights. Aztec tradition included human sacrifice in which jaguar-headed altars received the still-beating hearts of victims. The word 'jaguar' comes from Amazonia where Guarani Indians tell of a beast, *yaguara*, that attacks with one leap. The jaguar frequently subdues its prey in such a manner, killing quickly by biting into the skull or neck as opposed to strangulation, the preferred method of most large cats. The jaguar is the New World's most powerful predator, and it grows larger in southern Amazonia; some males measure eight feet from nose to tip of tail and weigh over 300 pounds.

This jaguar's title is *Lord of Olmec*, after the Olmec culture. Call him Olmec.

I remain yours faithfully,

Dr. E. Traboulay, Resident Zoologist and Conservationist.

Toward an opening in trees on the other side of the zoo, the *yaguara* was looking, and looking, a gaze as steady and penetrating as though he had sighted prey.

Had the *yaguara* been able to leap through the cage, through the air and into the trees and beyond, across the night sky, flying in a magical leap to what lay in the distance across the sea, he would come to the coast of South America. He would land on a long wide and beautiful beach, the moon lighting it as if its sand were made of salt or crushed diamonds. He would run along the beach, hearing the sound of waves, enjoying the scent of sea and the soft sand beneath his paws. Soon he would angle toward the jungle, running to its dark green billions of leaves tinted by moonlight. And there he would be.

Balam.

NIGHT RAIN

The land is dry. He walks slowly up the hill to the house, his shoes disturbing powdery earth among the stones. It is late, cool and the moon is high above him. There are no other houses around. He can see bits of quartz glinting on the road. The cliffs of another smaller island are dull cream, bare. Between the islands he sees moonlight on the sea, and a sailboat crossing the moonlight. A breeze stirs a poui he passes; the only sound; he can just hear it.

He stops to look at the stars. They are absent around the moon but light the rest of the sky. He stares at the sea for a while, begins walking again.

Higher up the hill, he sees a valley where the stone ruins of a colonial villa still stand. The moonlight shows the scorched land around the walls and pillars of the ruins.

He arrives at a gate. Two dogs, wagging their tails, come to him. He opens the gate, leaves it open, and goes with the dogs, stroking their long floppy ears, across the gravel driveway and into the garage, where there is a jeep. A watchman is lying on a wooden table. There is a bundle of cloth under his head. He is asleep, the garage light on over him.

He opens the door connecting the laundry-room and garage. The dogs whine. They look up at him and he holds their stare. Their eyes are large, limpid and brown. The dogs wag their tails. He enters the house.

In the kitchen, in cool darkness, with the combined star-and-moonlight visible through the shutters, he opens the fridge, gets his water bottle, and drinks fast. He sighs but is not tired.

A wind comes into the garden, a garden of scattered trees, crotons, cacti and bougainvillaea hedges. The acre of fenced-in land is bone-white in the moonlight; many of the plants, even some of the cacti, are almost emaciated. The bougainvillaea hedges bloom. He shivers. The sea is visible in the distance below; no moonlight there, it is darker and immense. He takes keys from his pocket and opens a wrought-iron door onto the verandah. He walks to the nearest hedge and picks some of the flowers, close to their petals. Then, walking quickly, he re-enters the house.

In the bedroom there is a young woman on the double bed. He sees one long bare leg, angled. She is hugging a pillow, an arm curved above her head. Her breasts, pale and protruding, are half-covered in moonlight. He rests the bougainvillaea flowers on the windowsill above her head. Through the window he can see the sailboat anchored in the moonlight, and someone, silhouetted, rowing a dinghy towards shore.

He carefully removes a packed duffle bag from beneath the bed and goes to the bathroom with it. He puts it behind the shower curtain in the bath, goes to the sink, washes his hands and face, brushes his teeth, undresses, then puts his clothes in the duffle-bag. Then he returns to the bedroom, and eases into the bed beside her. She senses him, and he moves closer for her warmth. He begins stroking her back, sitting up against the headboard. Soon he moves down along the length of her and hugs her. He holds her very close and kisses the back of her neck. Again and again. He can do nothing more.

The moonlight and starlight fade. The dogs trot on the gravel outside. A wind starts, building and building until he hears a low moan around the house. Now and then, as the wind moves them, sun-chairs scrape on the tiled floor of the verandah. He listens to the wind in the trees, the whine of the dogs, her interrupted breathing, and the creak of the roof.

Then he hears the rain, and listens, thinking.

She stirs, whispering to him, hugging him, moving against him for his warmth now, and kissing his hand.

It's raining just like you told me it would, she says. *I love the rain*, she says, rubbing against him. He almost does not hear her.

The rain… the rain, she murmurs.

She is asleep with her arm around him.

He listens to the rain for a long time.

NEAR OPEN WATER

The world of the living contains enough marvels and mysteries as it is: marvels and mysteries acting upon our emotions and intelligence in ways so inexplicable that it would almost justify the conception of life as an enchanted state.
   – 'Author's Note' to *The Shadow-Line*, Joseph Conrad

Adam had an idea.
He and the snake would share
the loss of Eden for a profit.
So both made the New World. And it looked good.
   – "New World," Derek Walcott

I

The house was built against a cliff cut into the earth so it could be cool and shaded and out of sight from the open sea. Level with the roof there are trees, and their land slopes upward to bushes and other trees that almost hide a wire fence. The grass there crackles underfoot. The dry season should end soon. On the house's smooth white roof, half-cylindrical plastic drains line the edges to collect rainwater and direct it to the cistern under the house. It has not rained for months. The house belongs to my cousin Jason.

There are times when I feel it's impossible to just walk away, to get on with it, as they say, to look forward to a future in which our memories have been relegated to the day-to-day details on a drink-stained postcard one sends to tepid acquaintances from the lobbies of tourist hotels.
   Will we let that happen to us? Will you?
   Remember me. Imagine me.

From the balcony of Jason's house – an area sectioned off from the living room by wooden green walls of horizontal planks and varnished wooden pillars – through the trees I can see small islands on the blue sea. Apart from the northeastern tip of one, they are untouched, looking as they did, I imagine, when they adjusted to the atmosphere after being pushed up out of the sea; many of the smaller uninhabited islands in the Lesser Antilles give this impression. The touched part of that one island, the biggest one visible, Crump Island, is a scar of earth, made by idiots who ripped the green away for some resort idea they had. Thankfully, I cannot see it from Jason's house. But if I go along the driveway, past where there is a scented plum tree shadowing part of the house, to where it widens circularly and is laden with rotting plums on the dark grey gravel, toward the dull-green gate at the end, then continue through the gate and turn inland, I come to a hill whose top allows me to see the scar. There're no other signs of human habitation: no cars, no houses, no sounds, nothing, no matter where I look, whether toward the smaller islands to the northeast, where the one with the scar is, or around what I can see of the main island. There's only the dirt road I walked up the hill on (it goes no further), and another dirt road that takes you several miles away from the house to a main road into town. From up there, Jason's house is hidden mostly by the trees and land above it. The scar can appear uncanny if I watch it long enough, against the blues of sea and sky.

Jason, who is on holiday for six weeks with his wife Kim, has a dog, Ojay, a white Alsatian. She was capricious, even growling at first, but I spent time with her so now she tolerates me. When I set the alarm at night, she seems to accept me a bit more each time, meeting me at the two-car garage, even accompanying me on my rounds, as if checking to see I'm doing it properly. She's been trained not to go within ten feet of any of the seven alarms after I set the system. In the morning it's just a matter of tapping in one code, and everything goes off.

Ojay is playful, rushing blue-grey herons that feed on little crabs and fish on the shoreline. The herons break into the air when Ojay charges, and she looks after them, a front paw raised, her ears at their straightest, while she whines, as if regretting the evolutionary path her species followed.

Are islands cursed for people like us?

This is intriguing: "an area sectioned off"? – You mean cut off, don't you? It's what happens here, isn't it? We've been separated. Why? Islands are cut off. Removed. Is that a clue? Write something else, please, for God's sake. Write about us.

And tell me: are you going to go and take a good look at that scar again? Why even mention it if you have no intention of doing so. What is it in the blue? And are you going to mention what you found on the hill?

Is this some sort of ecological lament? And what's this: "As if regretting the evolutionary path her species followed." Really, that Ojay's some bitch.

Tied to Jason's jetty are two boats. One belongs to his brother, and is called *Miss Lisa*. It's a biggish boat, the kind used for deep-sea fishing, with a hood on top, two powerful outboard Yamaha engines, and aerials. Blue and white, it points east, as do both the boats. The next boat is Jason's – a Boston whaler called *Rumrunner*, also blue and white and smaller than *Miss Lisa*. Jason's boat has a light, sharp look as it sits on the water. Once the Boston whaler picks up speed and the bow levels off – maybe I'm going to the island near Water Heaven – the island where there are stranded llamas because of a deal some local and American businessmen attempted – the whaler skims over the water like a flying fish. Not used to the climate, the llamas have been dying. With the air becoming heavy and still, and the great heat upon the land, I think the llamas, when they die, die with relief.

What is it that prevents you from looking closely at you and me, I wonder. What is it? I'm here, there, wherever you want. The Sahara dust sticks to my skin when I run in the afternoons. Imagine it. Then the rain will come and it will rain for days on end and the sky will be washed clean. The rains are here, people will say. Rain for days. We love the rain.

The future is the future and all we can do is to leave it open to possibility. Don't you agree? Don't you see?

There are mornings when it's difficult to write. At the long table on the western side of the balcony, next to the corner of the green wall that enables me to see the sea and islands, the difficulty of finding what I want to say discourages me. At these times the colours of the land and sea, the quality of light and the massive expanse of sea (nothing between here and Africa), help to connect me to a part of myself with which I'm uneasy, that gives me little faith in my work.

That day I went up the hill I saw what might be the problem, at least a sign of it. I found an iron, one used about two hundred years ago, maybe even longer, just an old heavy, rusted iron, compact and still intact, a blunt solid thing. It seemed so weapon-like. I imagined it must have pressed many clothes, the labour of slaves who worked in those outdoor kitchens and rooms away from the main houses. I wanted to dig; maybe there was more to find, but I didn't; it felt wrong somehow – I'm not sure why, perhaps because the land belongs to Jason. He should be the one to discover what's there.

I left the iron where I found it, and walked over the crest of the hill, where the vegetation is swept like hair blown back, lashed again and again by the wind, and then began the descent to the shore, where the mangrove thickets cluster (this area is about two hundred and fifty yards northeast of Jason's jetty). There's a rough path winding down steeply through the bush. I saw footprints there last week, bare feet.

Why do you go there? You leave the hill and descend into a pit of vegetation where the close heat and loamy soil are enough to swamp the air. The curiosity is interesting, but why not go elsewhere, the other side of the hill, for example, where the dirt road runs past the old sugar mills with the slave pits? You took me there once. Why don't you go to the beach cove at the end of the road, below the stone ruins of the plantation house? It, too, would get you away from Jason's house, away from the blue, boiling eye of the sky.

Swimming occupies an hour in the late afternoons. To swim earlier is dangerous. There was a documentary my sister mentioned (when she called from London) about the high increase in skin cancer. Do the work and be careful, she said.

I try to.

Lot of good she did us... This matter of faith, and the uneasy part of yourself – you leave it abruptly. No reflection whatever; you told me that's dangerous, that's what's wrong with the world – the neglect of history, and of selves, even. And here you are, guilty of it, refusing to take your own advice. Or is it the melancholy the sea brings to most of us? It can't be just that. What are you doing? It seems an act of destruction has begun, something like the llamas, no? Or that scar on the island you seem reluctant to gaze out at again from the hill. An erasure of some kind, an attempt, rather, on your part is in progress. All I know for sure is that you're there, and I'm here. But would you put it entirely that way? Ha.
    Got you there, didn't I.
    Like those llamas, you're in a dangerous climate.

The occasional airplane and boat pass silently in the far distance. But once, about three weeks ago, a boat larger than *Miss Lisa* came right down past Jason's jetty. I was at the long green table on the balcony, writing, or trying to, and by the time I heard it, the boat was there, just off the jetty, cruising slowly: *Mornin' Glory*, pure luxury. I'm constantly struck by how the people on such boats seem beyond the reach of the mundane things of this world. Three men were in the stern, with a woman in a black string bikini prowling the main deck. On the upper deck a man and woman sat at the wheel. They were all stylish-looking. The women looked bought. The trees that rise above the roof of the house hide the balcony from the water but allow me to see what's beyond; yet when one of the men looked at the house with binoculars, I stayed absolutely still.

Birds, dark and brown with short arrowhead-shaped beaks, a dab of red on their chests, visit the wood-plank railing on the balcony; some alight on the long table I sit at. They have a high-pitched chirp, and sometimes I'm startled. Ojay appears then, giving a bark and glare as they fly off to the plum tree by the driveway. She patrols around the house at a brisk pace, usually in the late afternoons or at dusk and dawn. At night, when I wake, I hear her on duty.

Hummingbirds, too, are frequent visitors. I watch their tiny, sabre-like beaks, their feathers the colour of dark jade and dark emeralds that shine as if drips of glistening oil have been delicately rubbed onto their chests and heads. I hear whirring sounds from their blurred wings: it's that quiet here, now the pre-storm weather has come. When there's breeze, and the bougainvillea rustles and waves bunches of red and peach flowers to bounce against each other, I can't hear them; today, I can.

You're distracted, all right. And I know you hear my voice as sure as the sea's before you. You made a mistake by sitting before the sea in your cousin's abandoned house to write. And who were those people in the boat?

Wait a minute. Wait. I see something now of what you're doing. Do you?

One day a hummingbird meandered through the bougainvillea growing above the barbecue pit at the western side of the balcony. I was sitting at the table on the porch whose steps come up from the circular part of the driveway. The porch is an open area, the floor concrete and rectangular, and sometimes I sit there because the sea distracts me – not that I can't see it from there: I simply don't see the horizon before me, just one island and its edges of mangrove. I was sitting there one day and saw the hummingbird hovering among the bougainvillea blossoms. It lacked the dart-like movements peculiar to hummingbirds. Its movements were in slow motion, and the wings didn't whir as fast as they should have. The bird seemed barely aloft in the fragrant, soft-red air of the bougainvillea. At moments it rested with a weary look, the sabre-like beak cast down, feathers without glossiness. Then I saw the small, tired, dark eyes, the nearly imperceptible lolling of the head and, for a hummingbird, the dishevelled fold of wings. Soon, though, it was back in the air, resuming in slow motion the still precise insertion of its beak into the bougainvillea flowers.

The details' subtle insistence on the inevitability of mortality tolls a bell, but for what, my dear? Or, who? Such focus could only signal a deeper marine melancholy. Is this why you so infrequently receive faith when you sit where you can see the open sea? The clouds piling above the blue eternity of sea and against the blue eternity of sky: gaze on that long enough… You see, it's all internal, dear, and external. You remember me in the blue; I know you do. Remember the three years we spent stealing away to hidden beaches during the week while the rest of the world laboured. On days of perfect weather we imagined we could live off the blue of sea and sky – and let's not forget the wine, cheese and crackers. We felt privileged to be alive on that long lovely beach with dense vegetation and bright beige sand when we laid our bodies out in a solitude as bounteous as a pre-Columbian landscape. We lay about nude and relaxed like natives awaiting the end of the world by cosmic forces. We had no religion. What we had were gods for our choosing. God of the blue, the sea, the air, the green mountains, the sand. Take your pick; invent another – the god of Sun and Sex, then.

And Memory and Imagination.

I am you and you are me and we are all – *both, rather* – together *goes the old Beatles' song. I'm crying. Or is it dying?*

Jason's jetty begins with earth and sudden slopes of rocks on either side, then a wider piece made of concrete and lined with narrow inch-thick planks of greenheart angled upwards so anything rolling across the jetty is unlikely to go into the sea. The screws supporting the planks are rusted, and in some places the planks are brittle. I had a casual foot on a plank one morning, Kim by my side. Jason was in the house. My aunt and her husband and their son Julian were in *Rumrunner*. I was carrying a cooler down to the boat when the plank slipped and I staggered.

Kim grabbed my arm and said, "Greenheart. I thought it would have lasted longer… Trees these days, they don't grow like they used to."

I didn't think about her words then. Only now, alone on the balcony where Jason and Kim offered wine, cheese, and fruit after the return from Water Heaven and viewing the llamas – only now do I remember her words. Now, during the quiet approach of twilight, Kim's words surface more and more with meaning.

Consider your focus on the jetty, the decay of wood, greenheart no less, and your attention to the shades of twilight.

Admit it: you're lonely, you love me, and you need me: me, myself, and I.

Us. You. And I have you, all right. So come and get yourself, then.

You suggest, like some sort of Port of Spain street prophet, an ominous future for Nature and, therefore, humanity. The gentle and kind Kim should have nudged you into the sea. You would have collapsed amongst all that gnarly coral and rock and bloodied yourself into a sobriety you desperately needed then and need now.

You're trying to be romantic, claiming to be arrested by a life other than ours. It's a lie. You are permitted only the Dark Romance of my absence, whose supreme image I shall direct your gaze to – heavenward, no less.

On the sea once, twice a week, a wind-surfer's sail flaps and I look up from my book or writing to see a boy leaning beneath the oblique wing, the shapely bulge of air firm in a red, yellow, and purple sail. He moves swiftly, and I regret I never learned how to do it; there had always been time, always the certainty that the day would come when the opportunity matched my liking. The young man out there began windsurfing, I imagine, when a genuine passion was possible, one that will sustain him and his windsurfing for many years.

The windsurfer fades away as I continue my work. The hard light has gone; the late afternoon tints are more to my liking, and I wonder if it's because I am getting older. The descent of light to twilight, and the sea becoming crepuscular… The world is different. At the end of the jetty, I collapse into cool, clear-green water. This colour lasts for fifty or so feet. After that blue takes over, a warm, close blue, close because the sand particles drifting make the blue visually impenetrable beyond seven feet. But the blue remains vivid, and gives the impression I'm swimming in aquamarine.

Well, I'm glad you know that exercise is helpful for depression. And that sweet bulge of sail: the curve of my hips, my breasts, and my unforgettable ass.

Your words, not mine.

And how appropriate to pine for the opportunities of lost youth, the time for a life-affirming experience. We fell in love during the furnace of our youth, so we bound ourselves together forever. You can't undo that, can you?

Remember your mother's aquamarine and diamond ring? The aquamarine was large, cumbersome, dwarfing the diamonds on either side of it. It's the same blue colour you swim in, isn't it? You once told me she said that if you were ever engaged to marry a decent girl she would give it to you for her. And your mother liked me, eventually – especially when your sister ran off to London to be with that rugby bum.

Your Caribbean ecological lament is dishonest, yet truth escapes somehow. Isn't that just how things are? Like water, truth gets into the most unlikely of places at the oddest of times. In dreams; when you cry in your sleep and wake to hear Ojay trotting around as she waits for what will inevitably come from the sea.

Regarding your condition, that other story you abandoned, the one with the old vagrant who scares the couple driving to the lookout by running out into the road, you abandoned it, didn't you, because you couldn't imagine beyond the scare he causes. Isn't that so? So now you write these paragraphs of flat-line observation, as if steadily looking at something and lying to yourself about how it makes you feel will solve the problem.

Let me tell you something: I am the Bitch and the Bitch is not dead. You can't deny what is true. Real. You should be writing about us, for God's sake, and in a way you are. But to represent me as a windsurfer sail is the sort of priceless asininity we should leave to our banana republic politicians.

Write: She lay in the lush garden of the old plantation house and watched her daughter's birthday party, the children with fluorescent-green baby iguanas resting on their arms, the iguanas feeding off the coolness of the evening, their eyes barely moving, as if subtly registering the curiosities of the night.

Restore me.

People disappear.

On certain days the current is not strong. The blue spreads out, dipping away into depths I feel a desire to explore but don't. The nearest point is three hundred yards away. The sound of my breathing through the snorkel is as familiar as the splashes my arms make. I've been doing this every afternoon for two months, and the results are good: I sleep better and have fewer nightmares. My work has improved, at least in this journal. Being at Jason's house has made life clearer, shown me the work I have left to do. I have to finish the writing, have to make a living somehow. But seeing how the economies of the world operate, seeing how they destroy the stability of countries and peoples, of families, individuals, I fear that my labour is being done for a broken world, a world which may have no use for it, or me. It prevents enthusiasm. The menace of history, perhaps.

A blue and silver fish, its blue denser than what I'm swimming in and sweeping up from its underside to fade into the silver dominating its top, curves out of another, hidden blue. The fish circles in front, mocking my progress locked at the surface, a sheet of white light marking the edge of its world. Nearer, the thin teeth are noticeable, pointing upwards on the outside of the mouth, like a deformed grin. The fish is large and circles me several times, slowly. In two months I've seen much marine life – barracuda, stingrays, leopard-rays, parrotfish, eels, and many others – including sea-centipedes, crusty-brown, ridged, lethal-looking lengths of Chilopoda – and most ignored me.

Further on, orange starfish, settled on the vegetation below, appear about one every fifteen feet. There are pimply bumps on the top of their tentacles and their centres look like neat, tiny mountain ranges in reddish sunsets. Their undersides are a canescent yellow, and down the middle of each arm there are short feelers, with tiny suction-cup tips, lining the sides of a long thin opening, a series of mouths. The arms tighten but do not fold when I bring one to my mask. The design of their arms engages me, how they taper to a blunt point from the thick centre, the delicate, precise movements of the feelers as they sense the sunlight and then recede with a quick, tucking-in movement into a cluster. I hold the starfish halfway between surface and seabed, and let go. The creature sinks, parachuting with five extended limbs, rocking from side to side. I catch it after a couple of feet, resting its small hard protrusions in my palm. Then I deliver the starfish to where I found it.

On my right, mangrove reaches into the water in curved forks. The water is green there, clear still, and calmer. It's near the end of the path that leads down from the hill. Where I'm swimming, the wind bounces on the water, making wavelets that obstruct the passage of air through the snorkel and the rhythm of my arms. I clear the snorkel with a furious spurt of air and kick harder, concentrating on my arms too, determined to get the burning sensation in my heart and shoulders that gives my body the deep peace I've become addicted to. Later, I want to sit on Jason's balcony after a shower of cool fresh water and reflect on the day. Ojay will condescend to be stroked around her perfect ears. But I must earn it, so I sprint for a while, glancing at the shoreline for direction.

The water is as warm as my blood and tempts me down to cool depths that make me wish I had gills. An article I read a few years ago said the possibility exists for us to create humans with wings and other animal attributes. Are gills possible? A barracuda angles on my left, and I realize fins would be, if not necessary, desirable.

I'm tired, swimming slower, floppily, looking up out of the water now and then to see how far away Jason's jetty is. The water off the end of the jetty has areas of hot and cold. As I glide through them, and by the crustaceous, green growths on the jetty shafts, with openings in which fish hide, an eerie thought occurs. It's the story of an eel a fisherman in the village told me – though he also said eels would not bother me if I left them alone – but I've seen movies that have done considerable harm to the reputation of eels, films showing the savagery of wildlife to man. It's all the fault of the undisciplined years of childhood, the easy access to stupid movies. Now trying to maintain a disciplined and focused mind for my work helps to control my emotions concerning eels.

And on our history together. And on imagining our future together, if such a thing exists.

Are you serious about "movies that have done considerable harm to the reputation of eels"? Sounds like some sort of radical environmental politics. And you would like to have gills? Fins? Scales? I can't wait for you to explain this. No doubt the sleek, canine Ojay is involved – she who seemingly "regrets the evolutionary path her species followed".

The ground floor of Jason's house is tiled in smooth squares of red-brown. There is a ship's bell at the bottom of a flight of steps.

The steps go up toward the northeast then turn one hundred and eighty degrees to the southwest. Up there is the balcony. Downstairs are the laundry-room and guest-room. The sliding door of the guest-room is unlocked and inside there are a few bookshelves, a bed, a sophisticated radio (one of Jason's hobbies), and a stack of newspapers and magazines. The shower is all I'm interested in. The water is cool and delights my skin as the film of salt is washed off.

Through the louvre-window near the ceiling I can see the cliff against the house, but hear nothing. The earth smells of iron and salt.

I walk out of the guest-room, and a dove, with streams of white on its chest, a sleek head and wet-brown eyes, flaps violently out of its nest above the archway leading to the jetty.

I stop. The sea is darker. Then, amid all the blues and promises of darker blues, amid the promise of night, I have a desire to swim once more.

No, sit back, get comfortable, but not too comfortable, and watch the outer dark come on and match your inner dark.

Shall we really return to the sea? Or do you wish to lift your gaze heavenward on this lavender evening? Of course you do. There. Can you see me in the mass of clouds above the horizon, where the blue has faded to lavender, and the promise of night is as certain as day and death?

Shall we return to the sea? Shall we, as Ojay seems to wish, surrender our evolutionary outcome? Or do we go to bed, rise early tomorrow, and begin writing about us?

The path appears to have been around for a while; it has the look of regular use. Walking down, coming to the shoreline, the light sea breeze dropping off and the full force of the day's heat gripping me, in the mangrove inlet I saw something I will never forget.

First, the boat: it was small and wooden, the colour of the mangrove roots and branches, old mossy splotches of greys and browns dried by sun and sea air. When it shifted a whole section of the mangrove seemed to shift too. So I stopped. And then I saw.

A thin, naked human form took life out of the shadows of the thick mangrove. It was attempting to get into the boat, fumbling with an oar; another oar stuck out at an angle above the bow. I did not recognize the sex of the figure until it turned – reluctantly, for she wanted to get away (now, I'm not even sure she was female) – and everything stopped, even my heart, as the mangled face looked at me. A jeer of deformed, protruding lower teeth, with the mouth at an angle, like a grimace of the most tremendous pain, made me gasp and step back. The eyes had a pure stark terror, their whites dashing across her face beneath the scraggly dark hair hanging over them to her neck and shoulders. Then she, or he, snarled, or what sounded like it. I realize now as I write, as she stepped back too, that she was more afraid of me than I was of her. But in shock, I took another step back and fell onto the path. I can't remember hitting the ground; all I recall is watching from there as the woman in the boat moved away, pushing on the mangrove roots with an oar. She looked at me, confident of safety, I thought, and that brutalized mouth seemed to grin.

I got up and ran up the path, scrambling like a terrified creature. I could not remove the face from my mind: the sudden confrontation with it had to work its way through. When I got to the top of the hill, I was trembling. Then it occurred to me to try and see where she might be rowing along the mangrove. But there was nothing to see; she must have been closer to the shore.

I began to walk back to the house, and about halfway there broke into a run, in the panic that the poor deformed woman or man might be trying to break into the house. Then I remembered Ojay, and rested, trying to calm my breathing.

Funny how accurately you observe what is before you… and yet, how little you see. That tormented demon-like person in the mangrove means something terrible happened, doesn't it? Of course it does. All demons, no matter what reality they inhabit, no matter what form they take, come from something. Do you see that, at least? And if that's the case, then won't something terrible happen again? Isn't it just a matter of when? And what? And who? If the past is not dealt with, if we neglect our history, our time together, if we refuse to look at things the way they must be looked at, then the future is cursed.

Everything is about to change. Trust me. Everything.

II

Ojay trotted across the porch as he slept through a nightmare. She was the wolf searching for him, hungry for all of the world and for all of time. The landscape rose and plunged like a stormy sea, and he could not go in any direction for more than a few yards: he fell, grabbed branches of trees and was tossed up and down constantly (could he fly?), even somersaulting off a branch to land heavily on the writhing earth, before being thrown up again. There was no sky, just the never-ending night of a cosmos devoid of stars: the wolf had eaten them all. The wolf came on, relentless, creeping low to the ground and exempt from the physics of the dancing earth. The demon of the mangrove rose in the air above him and consulted with the wolf. They spoke in loud whispers; he couldn't understand their language, but knew they were talking about him.

He woke sweating, heart pounding just as they were coming for him. He saw sunlight in exact, corn-coloured bars on the wall opposite his bed. He could just hear the sea splashing the land by the jetty. Ojay barked: it was all right. He got out of bed, stumbled, steadying himself on the bedpost. He tapped in the code for the alarm, dropped the remote on his bed, went out to the porch and climbed the stairs to the kitchen, not looking at the sea, sky, or the islands. As he made coffee, he ate five small sweet bananas, his body cooling, the sweat drying.

He stepped out onto the balcony with the coffee and saw a sky that looked so blue it seemed alive. Where it met the sea made a horizon perfect as an edge to the world: you could fall off into the blue and drift forever. Wind came off the sea; the trees alongside the balcony rustled and creaked; sunlight dappled the wood plank floor. It had rained in the night and he could smell the earth and the rot of leaves. He was still hungry. He remembered there were boiled eggs dusted with black pepper in the fridge.

At the table where his writing materials were – laptop, with journal and dissertation; long yellow green-lined notepads; green ink pens, blue ones too; books; shells and stones he'd collected months ago along the shore – he sat and sipped his coffee and waited for her voice to begin again, waited, gazing around at the sea and sky, the islands, turning in his chair to look upon the beauty of the world. But he heard only the day: the birds, the sea picking up in the wind by the jetty, the trees, and Ojay's enquiring bark as a great blue heron rose awkwardly into the air, as if about to break apart.

Soon the wind brought the sound of an engine; but his reverie blurred it from mind, just another boat passing. Then, like scalpel-blade reflections, light came through the leaves, flickered across his manuscript, and he looked out. The boat had slowed, so the sound of its engine was minimal. It was cruising up the channel, heading toward the house, the same boat he'd seen nearly four weeks ago, *Mornin' Glory*, its upper-deck cabin-window a flame of silver light. They (he assumed the occupants would be the same group of men and women he had seen the first time) would be formed out of the flame, apparitions arriving in this world as if from another. As the boat came on, once more its voluptuous luxury made him uneasy; he saw a man with binoculars again and heard Ojay growl below the balcony, as in the nightmare with the demon in the mangrove. But she was as yet unsure, waiting, an expertly trained animal ready to act, or not: the boat was not *yet* close enough to justify an attack. Information: it was what you needed in these situations; and that cost time.

Ojay waited. The boat came on steadily, its human forms more distinct now. In a matter of minutes Ojay would be on Jason's jetty, if that was the destination of the boat's occupants.

He shifted in his chair as if to rise, thinking both of the cold eggs in the fridge and trying to distinguish whether the women were on board. It was his first mistake: the time taken to indulge the thought, to act on the desire, and consider the result. By the time he'd looked out at the boat, scanned its deck and stern, and realised the women were not there, at least not on the exterior of the boat – so where were they? – fifteen seconds had passed.

Something was happening. He knew it now. Something had been happening for months, even before he came to Jason's house to recover after the disappearance. He got up and went to the kitchen, heard Ojay's growl resume and thought of shoes and eggs, though he wasn't hungry anymore. He bounded down the stairs. In his room he grabbed his running shoes, went back up to the kitchen, put the eggs in a bag, and ran to the balcony. The laptop he tucked under cushions on a sofa opposite the table, then he put his shoes on, tying the laces without looking at the task, peering through the trees at the jetty, seeing the boat coming alongside, three men on board wearing jackets in the early morning heat, baggy knee-length pants and dark glasses. Then two men were at the side of the boat, preparing to jump onto the jetty. He heard Ojay in the shadows beneath the balcony beginning to snarl, waiting for the moment they were on her territory. He dashed to the stairs behind the bougainvillea that connected to the drive-way, and leapt down four at a time, his heart beating so hard he could hear nothing else. He ran to the gate, his mouth scalded from the fire in his chest, hoping the bushes along the driveway would hide him. The gate's chain slid to the ground when he yanked it, and turning to close the gate so they would not see it open and get on his trail sooner, he saw Ojay white in the early sunlight, sprinting at them on the jetty with a locked concentration, low to the ground like a jaguar rushing its prey. She managed to leap at one of the men and both man and dog fell into the water. The other man reached into his jacket for his gun, turning and aiming down at the water between the boat and jetty.

Bent at the waist, he began running to the hill where he'd found the old iron. In the distance there were several gunshots. At the top of the hill he rummaged in the bush where he'd tossed the iron and lifted it out. Then he ran off the path into the bush and scrub, making his way down toward the cove half a mile away. He could see the sugar mill on the hill above the cove, and that was where he headed, out of breath, cutting his legs on razor grass, stumbling on rocks, and thinking about water and his life.

As he ran, keeping to where the vegetation and trees were thickest, he tried to think clearly. It wasn't him they wanted, surely they would see that, for the laptop, if they found it (and they would if they searched the house), contained nothing; it would release him; he was not responsible, or in any way connected with what they were after. What were they after? It must be Jason. But he shouldn't have hidden the laptop, for if they found it and read the journal, they might misunderstand. They'd realise he knew Jason was in Europe on holiday. So he'd been told. His phone – he'd stupidly left it in his room downstairs: it contained Jason's phone number.

He was connected to Jason, he had been in the house, Jason was his cousin, and Jason had met her, too. He didn't want to think about that; it would only confuse matters more. But he knew her and trusted her and they had no secrets – or had had no secrets: he didn't know what tense she was in, or where she was.

People disappear.

The heat increased, and the iron became heavy; he switched it to his other hand with the bag of eggs, wondering if the eggs would slow his fast-developing thirst. He usually had water after his breakfast coffee. The trees here gave scant shade, but he dared not stop. Soon they would be looking for him. They were most definitely searching the house now, and then they would come for him. He couldn't go far without going back for the car, and that was impossible. There was no one else around for miles. It could only be a matter of hours before they caught him, if that was their intention. He began to eat the eggs because he wanted strength: he was thinking of running to his aunt's house – and he needed to eat anyway. Then he thought the men would find the car keys, and while two would be in the bush tracking him, another would be moving quietly along the track in Jason's SUV. Maybe. He didn't know. He had to stop thinking. The eggs, warm now, were picking him up a bit, giving what felt like hope in the circumstances, but they didn't lessen his thirst.

He knew they would be able to see the ruins of the plantation house and the sugar mill from the hill, but it was unlikely they knew the area. Yet it seemed possible they had cruised back and forth along the coast of the island looking for Jason's house for weeks. He would chance it: get to the sugar mill and hide until night, then attempt jogging to his aunt's house.

The morning was quiet. He'd been trudging down through tall grass and past small trees, every now and then stopping for a few seconds to listen. As he came onto the shaded beach of the cove, glancing upward for a second at the branches covering him and wondering if it was possible to see this part of the cove from the hill, he saw a mongoose near the water, upright on its hind legs; it regarded him briefly, with an almost sympathetic curiosity, then fled. He sat, facing the water, resting on the still cool mixture of sand and mud.

The remaining eggs felt hot. He leaned forward and dipped the bag with them into the water.

About fifty yards to his right along the beach, the stone ruins of the plantation house's steps descended in disarray; it seemed there'd been an earthquake a long time ago. The trees there, their green still vibrant and lush, blocked his view of the higher part of the hill and the ruins up there, beyond which were the slave pits. Along the shore a clearing tunnelled a path through an increasing cluster of bushes and small trees. He tried to listen. The blood in his head was slowing, the sounds of the world returning. He felt drained running from the house. There were four eggs left, and he ate one. The gentle slap of water, the light wind in the trees: he listened to these sounds for several minutes.

Then anger overcame him; he stood up and decided he had to go back to the house; the men were mistaken: they didn't want him, he would say, nor even Jason. Whatever they were after he would help them get it. He had nothing to do with what they were about: he was a writer, poor, with a first degree in biology, the second in literature; he had attended Boston University. He was going to be a writer and teacher. Jason had allowed him to stay here, to work. And did they know there was a mongoose nearby, behaving strangely, observing him as if he were a distant relative? Most remarkable: surely a phenomenon to be observed and noted.

But he didn't move: his run from the house, the men with their guns, Ojay's attack and death replayed in his mind, fast.

He forgot the eggs and the iron as he began to run, muttering to himself, running toward the tunnel through the clustered bushes and trees. Now he would run along the shore for a ways, then turn inland to the right, pick his way up the hill to the slave pits, and there wait until night.

The mongoose scampered across the little beach and began rummaging through the bag of eggs.

III

Two men are walking slowly, now and then glancing behind them, through a landscape of dry cedar trees. The trees are still, the coral earth dusty. The morning has lost its coolness. The men are sweating. One man, stocky, in his early thirties, has a knapsack-cooler on his back, a Magnum .38 in his right hand, a green bandeau around his head. He wears Bermuda shorts and a pale-blue cotton jersey. The other man, taller, has an Uzi slung over his right shoulder, right hand clasped around the trigger area. The weapon points straight out in front of him at hip level. He wears a khaki shirt, a grey cap with the flap tilted up, blue jeans and sneakers. Both men are unshaven.

"Like he know how to walk, the fuck," says the shorter of the two. "I not seeing if he pass here."

The taller man, a bit older than his companion, hums. He isn't looking at the grass or the earth, but ahead at the sugar mill on the hill, both coming into view.

"Look there, nuh man. He could be hiding up so."

The shorter man looks and grunts.

"The mills have pits round them. I sure he hiding there."

"Is so? How you hear about that?"

"I read it in a brochure, at the hotel."

The shorter man says nothing. He looks around, grimacing, his discomfort evident to the other man, who shakes his head.

They both stop when they hear a noise, like a cough, and then step apart from one another off the path and crouch, hiding in the low bushes sloping down to the cove. They cock their weapons and wait.

A young man, sweating, is walking with purpose and wild expectation on his face. He is coming toward them, muttering, his sneakers stirring the dust. The shorter man stands and steps out onto the path, his .38 pointing at the young man. "Stop," he says. The young man starts, halts. The gunman has both hands on his weapon, right index finger on the trigger. "Everything fuck up," he says.

The young man is confused by this comment. "A mongoose," he says. "There's a very strange one back there," he indicates with his right hand, shaking. "I have to get my notebook." He begins walking again.

The taller man steps in front of him. "Wait." The Uzi is pointed at the young man.

The young man stops. "I'm not who you looking for," he says.

"Everything fuck up," the stocky man says.

"I just stay there. I write. You have to let me get my notebook."

"Don't move," says the taller man. "You going the wrong way."

"You must be the police. Come back with me and I'll let you in the house."

"Man, everything real fuck up."

"Where's Doreen? Have you found her? Where is she?"

The taller man looks at the shorter man; they are both a bit puzzled, but only for a moment. The taller man nods to his companion, who raises his gun and shoots three times into the young man's chest. He falls backwards, landing on his left side, an incredulous look on his sweaty face. "The mongoose," he sputters. "I have to get back to the house."

Both men laugh, but the taller one turns away. In a single graceful movement, the knapsack is off the shorter man's back, and he has a machete in his right hand. He puts the knapsack on the ground, grabs the longish hair of the young man, and with two expert blows cuts off his head.

The shorter man allows the head to drain before placing it in the knapsack, which he zips securely. He wipes the blade on the headless young man's body. While they walk away, the shorter man says, "He head heavy. Must be have plenty brains. 'I write. You have to let me get my notebook! Where is Doreen?'"

'His fiction is at once precise and evocative of landscape and the complex inner space of human situations. It moves with remarkable control across different layers of social class and ethnic diversity.'

– George Lamming

'When published, *Near Open Water* will make an important contribution to Caribbean Literature.'

– Lawrence Hogue

'Jardim is alive to character and social currents at once, and he is able to make me care about each. His dialogue is crisp, pungent, and his mastery of dramatic action – and of menace – is obvious.'

– Frederick Busch

'The sense of place is fabulous, a very complex sense of place, interweaving vistas of landscape and seascape, local fauna and flora, architecture, politics, inhabitants, history... all of which creates an atmosphere of longing and despair – despair at the impossibility of ever achieving what is longed for (the classic Romantic conundrum of setting for oneself a purpose that can never be accomplished, or worse, longing for a purpose, but what?). That lack of satisfaction – the sheer impossibility of ever achieving satisfaction – is wonderfully palpable throughout the stories... But the stories aren't Romantic as such – far from it; they play nicely with the disjunction between place as redemptive and place as punitive/purgatorial. The sense of foreboding in all of the stories is impelled by this tension, and by the political and social corruption that pervades them. In this sense, the work is "postcolonial" in the very best definition of that critical label.'

– Lois Parkinson Zamora